An Ada Picou Adventure

SHOWDOWN

Book III of III

A. B. Parr

1

Showdown: An Ada Picou Adventure

Written by A.B.Parr

Copyright © A. B. Parr 2023

All rights reserved.

Disclaimer:
This is a work of fiction. All characters, locations, and businesses are purely products of the author's imagination and are entirely fictitious. Any resemblance to actual people, living or dead, or to businesses, places, or events is completely coincidental.

Showdown

This book is dedicated to Leyla.

Showdown

CHAPTER ONE

M. Picou,

I regret to inform you that William has taken ill.

If you are able, hasten to us.

- M. Peace, Cerrillas

Ada Picou rode hard until she was all the way out of the Nebraska Territory, leaving the snow and blood behind her. Her mind worried about William and his health more than her own welfare. The roan had his head and tore Ada away from a winter full of death.

Together they cut through the snow, going faster as it became shallower on their route south. A murderer was ahead of her, leading her back to her ranch. She had hunted the Preacher into the hellish and snow-laden landscape of the Dakota Territory and now she carried the bounty set by the top general at Fort Albacrombie. Despite the change in circumstance, her goal remained the same:

To hunt and kill the man she knew as the Preacher.

Ada shook the last of the snow off of her shoulders and cursed the cold. "Ahmma ride that jackal down."

The roan chuffed as he broke through the snowbanks and into open earth. A warm thread in the wind found its way to Ada and her horse.

Revitalized, they increased their pace. Ada did not push the roan, but she did not hold him back as he loped across the countryside. The man that killed her family and that she had been chasing for most of her life was just before her.

As Ada rode onward, a farm appeared on the horizon. She pulled the roan up as fatigue worked over them both. "Ah guess we gotta head over that way." Ada's face tightened as she considered whether the Preacher was lying in wait. "Hell with it," she grumbled as she tapped her heels and gave the reins a flick.

Weary in the saddle and with lips dry and cracked, Ada narrowed her eyes to slits as she rode toward the farm that stretched far ahead of her surrounded by miles of rolling land full of budding grass. A stiff wind from the north bit at Ada's neck and she hunched low and tucked her chin into her worn layers.

Casting her eyes across the range, she noted the newness of the farm. Wooden buildings were yet to be bleached by the sun and Ada could smell the freshly cut lumber. Stumps, not yet burned from the landscape, littered the barnyard. Large stones jutted out in various places and the people living there had started piling them near the barn, likely to use as building materials.

It was the first time she had crossed people since leaving Fort Albacrombie in the Dakota Territory. Ada leaned back and considered her position. "Bag's runnin' light." She ran a hand over the roan's croup and tapped her nearly empty saddle bag.

The horse stamped his foot.

"Ah now, yer ready" Ada said. "Jist don't wanna catch no bullet again." Her hand absently went to her thigh and the spot where she could still feel the puckered flesh through her denim. "Alright," Ada tapped her unspurred heels to the roan as they closed the final distance.

The horse rode slowly over to the dark, freshly tilled soil and chuffed.

Ada imagined the dirt held the charred remains of wood scraps and night soil. A farmhouse and a barn loomed on the opposite side of the barnyard. There was a man and a woman in the field and the farmer stiffened as Ada she approached.

The farmer stopped the plow he had been working the land with and bellowed, "Hold girl," to his mule. He released the worn and smooth handles of his plow and called to Ada, "Don't get much folk 'round here." He spoke curtly, with a suspicious eye and a beetled brow. He lifted his chin to Ada and shifted his body to square off with her. "You lost?"

Ada took in the farmer's sour look and rigid frame. She shook her head but declined to speak.

"We don't want to no trouble," the farmer gestured with his head for her to move along and made a point of picking up a nearby ax. He was broad and muscular, and had a red, wiry, wild beard wrapped around his face.

"Jist passen through," Ada said, as she stopped the roan at the edge of the field. "Ah ain't here to be no trouble. Jist want to see if y'all would trade some foodstuffs for these here hides." She patted a folded layer of animal skins that lay right above the dock.

Movement from the house caught Ada's eye as a young boy darted about the shadows inside the home. Ada glimpsed wheat-colored hair matching that of the woman standing behind the farmer. "Yer lucky to be here," Ada spoke absently as she leaned forward in the saddle and rested her arms on the horn while scanning the buildings for trouble. "There ain't much snow this far south of the Dakota territory," Ada added casually.

The man relaxed his posture a bit, but eyed Ada warily.

"Ah ain't smelled spring in a coon's age." Ada took a deep breath.

"Still cold around here," the man spoke and looked north. "That wind's got a bite and the ground is still hard," he added as he rolled a pipe on his lip. "You alone?"

Ada nodded. "What are ya plantin'?"

The man seemed taken off guard by the question, but shook his head when he spoke, "Greens." He took the pipe out of his mouth and spat onto the hard, dark earth. "Nothin' to concern yourself with. You should ride on, stranger." He stood proudly as he looked over his land.

"Got ya a real nice spot sheltered from the wind," Ada added.

"Had some snow, but it didn't last." The man looked back to Ada. Suspicion darkened his eyes, and he crossed his arms.

Ada sat on the roan in silence and did not move.

"Keep riding," the farmer spoke abruptly.

Ada started, "Hey, now. Ah didn't do y'all nuthin'—"

The man spat again. "And ya won't."

The farmer's wife held up a rifle with the barrel pointed at the ground. Her form was partially hidden by the big redheaded man.

Looking around, Ada confirmed once and for all that she saw no trace of the man she hunted. "Alight, ahmma goin' off," Ada huffed. She pulled at the reins, steering her red roan away from the homesteaders.

Slowly, and sitting low in the saddle, Ada rode her way past the partially tilled field.

"Wait," the woman called to Ada from behind her husband. The farmer turned in surprise, as if he had forgotten she was behind him. She set the rifle butt down and rolled the barrel in hand. Her hair, tight and pulled back, caught the sun and gleamed a radiant gold.

Ada pulled up at the reins and shot the other woman a questioning look.

"Now Thomas," the woman said, while walking toward Ada. She put out a hand to stop the man from following her.

The farmer's face twisted and reddened in anger, but the farmer's wife ignored him.

The golden-haired woman kept her gaze on Ada. "We don't want any trouble, but you hardly seem fit for it."

Ada felt the scrutiny of the other woman and sighed. "Yeah, ah ain't too much of nuthin' lately," she said with a shrug. She recalled how she'd looked the last time she spied her reflection in the water and her eyes were dark with exhaustion. Shifting her weight in the saddle and looking south, Ada tightened her hands on the reins, ready to ride off.

The farmer's wife looked Ada up and down. Arms crossed and with a kindly eye, she observed, "You look to me to be tired and hungry."

The man named Thomas shook his head slowly as he rested the head of the ax on the ground. It was a long-handled ax that displayed signs of much use. The husband and wife shared a look, and an expression crossed their faces that Ada could not interpret before Thomas eventually went back to the plow with the intention of completing the row.

Ada raised an eyebrow in confusion. "Yea mam, we're plum beat." She cast her eyes to Thomas and watched the man work as she continued, "But if we ain't wanted round, well," she tilted her head at Thomas as he looped the ropes about his frame.

The woman with the golden hair called out, "Thomas, she doesn't look like anything dangerous."

"Ah ain't," Ada sighed as she rubbed her wounded leg, "no more, at least."

Thomas nodded to his wife begrudgingly and clicked to get the mule pulling.

"Come on down," the farmer's wife turned and gestured to the house. Her face lightened, and she looked eager to talk.

Ada stepped out of the creaking saddle and led the red-spotted horse toward the house, where there was a spot of grass near the stoop that the horse helped himself to.

"We don't see many strangers in these parts. Especially women. My husband thought you were a vagabond or bandit." The woman stood on the porch and looked at the great rolling hills in the distance. She was wearing a simple home-spun woolen dress with a cream-colored pattern peeking out from underneath. Ada recalled there was a matching pattern on the farmer's shirt.

"I'm Rory, Thomas is my husband." She pointed to the barn. "You can stable your roan in there," said Rory.

"Good to meet ya mam," Ada tipped her hat and led her horse the rest of the distance to the small barn. "Thank you," she added as she walked. Her limp bothered her, but there was no way to hide it.

A sharp stab in her thigh made her wince as she led the horse. Wearily, and still wary at the turn in attitude from Rory and Thomas, horse and rider made their way to the barn.

The red roan whinnied in excitement.

"Alright, alright, let me git you settled." Ada removed the girth and saddle before placing everything carefully on the stall's wall.

There was no old dust in the barn, the wood was freshly cut, and the smell tickled at Ada's nose. "New place," she said, as she also noted the absence of rust on the nails and hinges.

Filling a water bucket with fresh well water from the pump outside took Ada longer than she was used to. Favoring one leg, she carried the pail awkwardly and lost a third of the water on the way back.

"Git some rest, boy." Ada stuffed a flake of hay into the wooden trough before the horse. She rubbed him down with a burlap sack as Rory entered the barn.

"I found this here. Can I use it?" Ada asked.

Rory nodded and put her hands upon one of the posts. "Don't mind Thomas, he just doesn't take to new folks." Rory shuffled her feet.

"Ah imagine y'all don't git many folks out this way," Ada observed.

Rory shook her head and looked around the barn, a look of pride on her face. "Especially recently," she added with a tilt of her head. She held Ada's gaze for a moment, backed by the swiftly setting sun.

"No break for us, is there?" Rory eventually asked Ada, while smiling softly.

Ada shook her head. "Nah, always got somethin' to keep us busy. Specially you, I'll bet, with that little fella." Ada gestured to the house.

Rory's eyes narrowed. "You riding alone?" Rory looked back at the horizon.

Ada nodded and quietly finished rubbing down the horse.

"Where are y'all from?" Ada asked, her interest genuinely peaked.

"Scotland," Rory answered clearly. She had a faraway look upon her face before a horsefly buzzing by her face broke Rory free of the spell of memory. "Darn these pests," Rory said.

Ada chuckled, remembering of the swarms of misquotes back home in the Atchafalaya. "If y'all ever git down to Attakapas ah'll show ya some big suckers. Ya ever seen a roach the size of a mouse?" Ada asked with a wry smile dancing on her lips.

Rory shivered and shook her head. "Where on earth kind of place are you from, Ada?" Rory asked.

Ada adjusted her hat and smiled. "Born in Louisiana. Living on the Atchafalaya ah seen some things."

Rory puckered her brow. "That is an awful long way off. We left Scotland and our family behind. Did you leave your people behind as well?"

Ada looked at the ground as the weight of loss pressed into her. "Nah, ah'm the only one left and I ride alone."

Rory gave Ada a worried look.

The roan whinnied happily nearby.

Rory chuckled. "I like you. I told Thomas you would be okay."

The corners of Ada's lips turned down and her brow tightened, her confusion evident upon her face.

"Ah don't follow," Ada questioned as she patted the dust from her hands.

Motes of sawdust went adrift where they caught the fading light as a supernatural-feeling emerged with the shift in conversation. The warmth in the barn that had penetrated into Ada's bones lessened with the approach of night. Ada's nose, thick with the smell of animals and hay, picked up the scent of something acrid and sour. Outside, the calm, silent, and peaceful land turned ominous.

The two women stood looking into each other's eyes as a moment passed.

Rory brushed aside the topic with a shake of her golden locks and brushed it off with a wave of her hand. "Don't worry over it, it's time to get supper done."

At that moment the small boy pushed through the door and scurried into the barn. "Ma, I'm hungry." He hid from Ada behind his mother but peeked at Ada all the same. "Pa is inside."

"Thank you, son." Rory gestured to the house. "Come along miss. . . what do people call you?"

"Picou, Ada Picou."

"Miss Picou, come and join us for supper."

Ada sighed deeply, nodded, and leaned back on her heels. "After you, mam."

Rory had apparently been slow-cooking salted venison for a stew since early that morning. She added a pot of beans to the stove and warmed some bread in the oven while Ada darned a shirt she had kept stowed in her bedroll that was in desperate need of repair.

"Good stitch you have there," Rory observed.

Ada shrugged. "Can't always get it to go with the grain. My Ma was right good at it."

Thomas sat nearby and was cleaning his tools while watching the woman from Louisiana work. "You've really no man with you?" Thomas blurted.

Ada stopped her repairs and looked at the door for a moment. "Not out here. Ain't got nobody out here. Got a place in the south, a ranch, over in the New Mexico Territory." The words rolled out of Ada without her thinking. Her heart beat faster as she continued, "Got somebody waiting for me there. A man by the name of William."

Rory threw her husband a harsh glance when she heard the strain in Ada's tone.

Thomas shrugged and went back to his cleaning.

Ada joined the family at the table when the meal was ready. There was a thick layer of tension inside the small house that left the occupants' little elbow room.

Rory spoke to her son, "Duncan, pass Miss Picou a slice of bread."

Frozen, the boy did not stir. He avoided looking Ada in the eye.

Ada wondered what the boy was on about as she chewed her food slowly. Every bite was a delight to Ada, a sentiment she felt the need to share. "Home cooked food's as rare as hen's teeth," Ada said as she reached over and retrieved her own roll. Nothing else was said until the food was completely eaten.

Thomas turned to Ada after the meal as he packed his pipe and asked, "What brings you out here?"

Ada felt the man's sharp eyes scrutinizing her thoroughly. "Headin' home," she spoke softly and sadly while offering a weak smile. Her eyes wandered to the fire-filled hearth as she thought about William and the ranch.

Thomas nodded his large head in an unspoken understanding of her need for home.

"William your beau?" Rory chimed in.

Ada shrugged and looked around the room while doing her best to avoid their waiting eyes. "Somethin' like that," she answered with a half nod and shrug.

A quick look passed between the married couple. Rory smiled silently as Thomas lit his pipe.

"How did you end up here, heading south, if you're from that there New Mexico Territory?" Thomas's face glowed in the light as the tobacco in the pipe burned.

"I was hunting," Ada answered, her lips tightening to a thin white line.

Thomas shook his head gently. "Those pelts you got don't seem enough of a draw," skepticism was clear in his voice.

"Oh, Thomas." Rory went a light pink with embarrassment.

"Nah, he's right. The animals was jist part of it." Ada paused and looked deep into the flames dancing in the hearth. "Ah was huntin' a bounty." Ada paused before adding, "still tailin' him."

The corners of Thomas's eyes tightened for a moment before he asked a fresh question. "How far have you traveled? I can't place your accent."

Ada appreciated the change in topic. "Louisiana. Ah grew up maybe a hundred and forty miles from New Orleans," Ada stated.

The boy's eyes went large and round like saucers as Ada told tales of her travels.

Rory patted the boy's shoulder. "Don't stare. It's rude."

"You've gone so far. It's not as far as Scotland, but for one person," the child mumbled in shock.

"My boy likes maps," Thomas said with a hint of pride in his voice.

"Alright, what sort of maps?" Ada directed at the boy.

Duncan squirmed out of his chair and ran over to a small chest. When he returned to Ada's side, he was carrying a piece of paper and handed it gingerly to her.

"Well, hot smack a rabbit," Ada smiled at the landmarks and detailed nature of the boy's drawings.

"This here is our farm," he pointed to a spot on one of the maps.

Ada nodded. "Ah kin see that. Ya got all the little details in here. Even those stumps I saw when I rode in."

Thomas grumbled, "I'm getting to those. You'll have to make a new map in the fall, boy." Changing the subject again, Thomas said, "My father fought in the war. He carried a gun for Mr. Lincoln." The farmer then drew on his pipe and goaded Ada a bit more. "He fought and he won," the man said. There was a noticeable pause as he watched for his guest's response.

Ada gave him none, and the room fell silent.

"What bounty's so big it brings you so far from either home, Miss Picou?" Thomas asked when Ada did not take his bait.

Ada tensed and clenched her jaw, but was ready for the question. She would have asked him the same if the roles had been reversed. "The man ah'm huntin' is wanted fer murder. There were a few murders committed up round Fort Albacrombie."

Thomas and Rory exchanged a quick glance through tight eyes.

"A Confederate bounty hunter eating at my table," Thomas said, his voice dripped with disdain.

The edges of Ada's jaw pulsed silently, and she rubbed at a callus on her left palm.

Rory's eyes widened as the electricity in the room sparked between Ada and Thomas.

"Ah've imposed enough Mister—" Ada stammered.

"Wilson," Thomas mouthed the word slowly and eyed Ada.

"Mr. Wilson, thank ya and yers fer showin' me kindness and fer dinner." Ada stood from the table and braced herself on the sturdy chair, the glow of the fire flickering across her face and reflecting in her cool eyes.

The large and weathered man pursed his lips, seeming to come to a decision about something. "You can sleep in the barn," Thomas said as he walked over to the stove where he lost his gaze in the embers. The red and golden lights dimly danced across his face. "Fire is a dangerous and beautiful thing, isn't it?" he mused as he gazed into the depths of the flames.

"Surely is," Ada agreed quietly after a moment.

Thomas turned to her, met her gaze, and spoke firmly, "Only when it's controlled though." His brow was furrowed and his body was taut as he gestured to the door with his head.

Ada looked at Rory, and the other woman nodded. A tight-lipped nod was all Ada could muster for the couple.

All the talk died as the flames dwindled.

Ada thanked the Wilsons again for the meal and awkwardly jerked open the old front door that was not quite square in the frame.

A silent velvet night greeted Ada as she crossed the barnyard on her way to the barn. An all-encompassing and peaceful calm had blanketed the farm after the sun set.

"Y'all doin' alright," Ada observed as she passed a small chicken coop with a dozen sleeping hens perched on a long and narrow branch. A rooster flanked the line and beat his wings at Ada as she passed. She paused again to look at the two pigs snoring in the soft, damp earth and leaned on the fence while she took in the sty. "Been a while since ah been round pigs. Y'all still stink, but lord it smells like home." Ada used her sleeve to wipe at her face.

The wind had lightened up after the sun went down and left the air heavy and still. The stars hanging in the sky filled Ada's vision when she glanced up.

"Too many." Ada's head spun as she looked back toward the solid ground at her feet and walked into the barn. A horse belonging to the farmer snorted at Ada as she walked by and she stopped to pet his soft nose.

Her roan nickered nearby.

"Ya jealous, boy?" Ada smiled to herself at the affections of the animals. Her thoughts soon returned to the couple working the homestead.

"Seem decent enough. Thomas'n that boy was mighty jumpy. Why'r they on edge?" Ada thought over the dinner and could detect nothing unusual. "So his daddy was a Yank. What of it?" Ada thought of her father and recalled the smell of the peppermint leaf he carried in his pocket. "War's over. Done is done." A feeling of guilt cascaded over her, but she could not determine its source.

Ada found an empty stall by her loyal red roan and laid her bedroll on some loose hay before settling on the use of her saddle for something to rest her head on. As she settled in, a thick tabby cat darted from the corner and leaped above Ada onto the beams.

"Whoa now, ah ain't gonna git in the way of ya and yer rats," Ada spoke softly.

The cat sat high above her and gazed down at Ada in mild interest.

Moving slowly so as not to startle the watching animals, Ada lowered herself as soreness and pain coursed through her. She cursed her body and the limits it put on her. She felt for the flask in her pocket and fingered her father's initials engraved upon it. No rye, or rum, or bourbon, but the feel of it in her hand brought her comfort.

Ada drifted off to sleep to the sounds of her horse snuffling for more hay.

In her dreams, she could feel the dry desert air roughing her skin. The sounds of cicadas wrapped her in a blanket of wild music that made her ache for home. The familiar feeling of mud sucking around her boots pulled at her thoughts. Ada dreamed of the dry land in New Mexico and the swamps of Louisiana, combining her memories of her two homes into one. In her dream, her dog barked and she reached down and felt his coarse scruff.

She awoke the next day to a pre-dawn darkness, disheveled, and in a body that ached all over.

"Is he alright?" Ada wondered about William even before thinking of the Preacher as she sat up and centered herself on her present circumstances.

Still in her bedroll, Ada heard someone moving around in the barn. Standing up slowly, her muscles taut and ready, she peered into the darkness.

"Up already, I see," Thomas said as he lit a lantern hanging from a beam. The golden light illuminated the concern on his face. "I come out here early to set for the day." He was talking casually, but kept as wary an eye as ever on Ada.

Ada pulled herself the rest of the way up and stretched.

"Spring is coming and I want to be ready," Thomas said.

Ada nodded and recalled her father. "My pa was the same."

Thomas nodded his approval as his face softened. "Nothing like having your own land and making something with it." He paused and looked at Ada and gestured to her horse. "You'll be heading out."

Thomas's words held no the hint of a question.

Ada leaned against the stall's wall and grumbled as she rubbed her face, "Yea, ah gotta job ta see through."

Thomas stood still with one hand braced against a post. "He came through here."

Ada's creased brow showed her confusion. She held her breath and steadied herself in the cool morning air, bracing herself for whatever would come next.

"We don't want no trouble." Thomas adjusted his marbled and flat-brimmed hat that was frayed with wear. "Your bounty rode through here a few weeks ago."

Ada stood in silence, her face going pale as her eyes tightened.

"He set us all on edge from the start," Thomas spoke quickly and low with a tinge of fear in his voice. "The boy just started talking again." He gestured toward the house without looking away from Ada and sighed. "I'm actually surprised Rory invited you in. When we saw you riding up, well, we didn't know what to think. I thought you might have been with that man or more of his ilk. It was as much a surprise when you turned out to be a woman, and riding alone no less."

Ada worried her lip and peered around the barn in search of some answer she knew was not present.

A moment of silence between the two was broken by the crow of the rooster.

 Ada blinked as if startled from a dream. "Did anything happen?" Ada ventured, "Did he do anything to y'all?" Venom dripped from her voice.

Thomas wrung his hands and looked at Ada with a grave

expression that aged him far beyond his years.

"We will live," Thomas stated. "He told us you were coming. I thought he was mad. No women would be riding down this way alone. He spoke like a church man, sure of himself. We didn't believe a word of what he said. Sent him packing as soon as he stopped talking. Tried to at least. I'm no hand with a gun. Not for killing folks." Thomas's hands shook, and he started to sweat.

Through it all, Ada listened with an expression cold and steady as the barrel of a pointed gun.

"That man told us he was going to New Mexico to burn it all down." Thomas fumbled his words, "I-I'm sorry, he told me to kill you. He was armed and had a cold, dead look in his eye. I knew he'd a shot at me and Rory. She was stove up as soon as he walked in the door. Duncan hid under the bed, but that man knew he was there. Kept pointing his gun at the bed and making threats." Beads of sweat covered Thomas's brow despite the morning chill.

The two stood in silence in the barn, neither one daring to make a move. The air was still and the animals, sensing the tension, did not stir. Electricity leaped from Thomas to Ada and back.

Ada held Thomas's eyes and sought his intent, but Thomas crumpled instantly under her intense gaze.

Thomas's shoulders sagged at a loss. "He said he would kill my family."

Ada watched as the weight of worry took its toll on Thomas's bearing.

Thomas shifted his weight and Ada knew the lunge was coming. She pivoted as he leapt at her and caught only air. Still turning on her boot toe, she snapped out a left to the back of his head.

Thomas stumbled from the strike, but caught himself in the stall and turned to Ada.

In that time, Ada had tightened her belly and brought her arms in front of her face. She held her head low as she took the hit to her clenched stomach, delivered by Thomas's left fist.

Ada's body almost lifted off the ground as the air flew from her at the strong man's strike. He grabbed for the breathless Ada as she dropped both hands hard to each side of his throat.

Thomas's head lolled, and he staggered as Ada slammed his forehead with a hard right. Before he could regain his balance, Ada struck a left to his trachea. The large man fell to his knees with a thud while clawing at his neck as he struggled to get air.

Ada slid back on her toes and narrowed her eyes at Thomas as he fell forward and caught himself with both hands and gasped out, "No more." Blood dripped from his split forehead into his eyes and he heaved to catch his breath.

When he looked up, he found himself on the barrel end of Ada's gun.

His voice shook, but he still managed to say, "I ain't no killer."

He held up his large and calloused hands, stained by the soil, in supplication to Ada's judgment.

Ada walked to stand before Thomas, gun still drawn. She holstered her weapon and stated, "He's evil, ah know yer jist wantin' to keep yer family safe." Ada grumbled deeply and rubbed at her belly while thinking of the bruise that would blossom there in the morning.

"Get him," Thomas finally said, "please," he added. Worry drove his eyes to his front door and the innocent family within. "Rory wouldn't poison you. Duncan was torn." Thomas dropped his eyes to the ground and stood slowly, his shoulders sagging in defeat.

As Ada walked over to her roan, she patted Thomas's shoulder. "Ah'll git him. He won't be this way again." She gave Thomas a tight and determined nod as she retrieved her tack. "Ya got a good left upper, but yer feet were off by a Texas mile."

A slight grin split Thomas's face and he pushed his hands into his pockets.

The white morning sun had paled the blue sky by the time Ada saddled her speckled roan. The horse was not ready to ride, and she had to work the girth to get it tight. She didn't admonish him though, she understood.

"Gettin' back to work, boy," she said as she led him out of the barn. Rory approached her with a package in one hand and a cup of coffee in the other. "Cat head biscuits and a few slices of salt pork," Rory said as she handed Ada the tightly wrapped bundle of brown paper. She placed a hand upon Ada's arm, her face tight in unspoken apology and guilt.

Ada nodded and held her eyes. "Ya gonna grow old enough ta pass this place on ta yer boy, and him on ta his boy."

She looked past Rory to where Duncan was hiding in the shadows of the opened door. She offered him a half smile, and he responded with a small wave before darting away into the shadows of the house.

Ada drank a swig of the coffee and placed the wrapped food with the little she had left. Handing the tin cup back to Rory, Ada smirked and tipped her hat. "Much obliged Mrs. Wilson." Ada slid her hard and worn boot into the stirrup and stepped into the saddle, wincing from the pains both old and new.

After lifting her chin to Thomas as he emerged from the barn rubbing his head, she clicked and gave her reins a shake.

The red roan cast a long shadow in the pale sun. They rode southwest from the homestead without looking back, the smells of the farm eventually fading into the distance. She could imagine the family watching her leave as they lightened with the relief of her departure, hopeful not see either her or the Preacher again.

CHAPTER TWO

Ada Picou sat in the saddle with shoulders back and her head high. She tried to ignore the old wound in her thigh that meandered between an itch and a burning sensation. The old sawbones at Fort Albacrombie had done well when he fixed Ada up after she'd been shot twice.

"Ah ain't lost the leg at least," Ada mumbled to herself as she recalled her father's stories of the war and the limbs he had seen lost. Her hand strayed from the reins and she rubbed at the persistent wound. The muscles had been torn apart and her gait would never be the same. "Ain't no amount of arnica fixin' this," Ada sighed in exasperation as she looked over the land before her.

Rolling hills with shallow valleys extending to the horizon filled her weary gaze. Tall and ancient trees whose wrinkled bark gave a wizened appearance dotted the landscape. The pecan trees rustled, their buds just starting to unravel as green peeked out and caught the sun's light. The trees stood much higher than Ada, some over sixty feet tall. They served as lone sentinels in a barren land.

The Preacher in black had obviously passed this way and was leading Ada south, so she kept a wary eye out for danger. The Sioux of the Dakota Territory she had left behind had informed her she would be crossing Pawnee and Arapaho land. Hunting parties and villages would be easy to spot, but the scouts would only be visible if they wanted to be seen. It was a crapshoot with the Preacher; Ada could not predict his ways.

Thomas and Rory had pointed Ada in the general direction of a lightly used road. There was not much to mark it aside from the faint trail it cut through overgrown scrub grass. Ada was not familiar with the terrain around her and stayed on the path etched by old wagons and weary mules.

Ada imagined the people that would have used this road when they migrated from the mighty Mississippi to this unforgiving land of hard-earned spoils. The long and slow hours turned to a haze of days as she made her methodical way south. Eventually, the land changed and both Ada and the roan noted new signs of life as the winter reluctantly gave way to spring.

On their way south, horse and rider encountered a few travelers whose wagons were loaded with goods. However, these folks were not traders.

"Where are y'all headed from?" Ada called out to one family.

"Carolinas," responded a man who had stopped for but a moment to answer.

There were not many in number, but Ada surmised them to be fierce and hardy. "They'll need to be to make it out here and beyond," she said to herself.

There were even a handful of craftsmen among the people in the wagons Ada surmised whenever she spotted their tools strung along the boards of their wagons. Every last person, men and women both, was looking to succeed through hard work where their luck had failed them back home.

Aside from an occasional shouted greeting, Ada knew she would do well not to get too close to any travelers after her encounter with Thomas and Rory.

That quaint little family in the Nebraska Territory had been tainted by a visit from the Preacher. Ada knew he was out there somewhere ahead of her, and she wanted to avoid incidents and accidents.

"Gotta keep movin' and don't talk to nobody," she told herself as she rode past a couple of small cozy homes whose freshly cut wood filled Ada's nostrils.

The roan nickered to Ada after several hours of nonstop riding.

"Ah know, boy. Yer wantin' to socialize and rest. We will," Ada sighed, "eventually."

Ada ached to go into those homes and feel welcomed, but she knew they were not for her. Another ache that was far greater pulled her south. Ada knew where the Preacher was headed. She had to get to William.

"Ah've gotta end this." Ada gritted her teeth as she rode on without knowing if the pull she felt in her belly was for revenge or something else.

Just as Ada was relaxing in the saddle, she noticed the fluttering of colorful rags in the distance. Drawing the reins tight, she stopped the roan in the road. Peering through narrowed eyes she realized she had come across a small trading post deep in the Nebraska Territory. What she saw was not a building as she expected, but rather a post made in the hollow of a hill.

After a moment of scrutiny, Ada let her horse meander in the direction of the flags. They curled and whipped in the wind, occasionally snapping in a gust. As she rode closer, she was startled to hear the flat pop of gunfire from the strange outpost.

A man on horseback flashed west and left behind a cloud of dust in his wake.

Ada froze for a moment and cursed. "Was that him?" she hissed into the wind. Ada loosed the reins and gave the leather a slight flick, driving the roan at a canter in the direction of the odd structure.

As they approached, the post, Ada could see that it was indeed built right into the raw and sloping ground. A large wooden door, framed with heavy pecan timbers, sat at the face of a grass-covered rise. Ada saw no windows or roofing, just earth and wood. Topping a pole in the earth above the trading post flew torn strips of material whose colors had dulled from flying in the sun.

"Ah mighta missed this spot if not fer them markers wiping about," Ada spoke to herself and nodded to the wisdom of the bleached strips of cloth caught in the wind.

The echoes of the shot long gone, eerie silence greeted Ada as she rode up to the post. One large door opened out to a well-worn area of hard-packed gray earth.

Hopping down, Ada's boots only dented the top layer of soft dust that had settled over the dry earth. Ada tethered her red roan to the hitching post outside the building where there were two other horses which both looked old and worn to Ada's eye.

Ada limped her way toward the structure with her Colt in one hand while cautiously keeping her eyes peeled for danger. Her stomach growled and she frowned. Her supplies were low and her curiosity was high, but right now she could not afford distractions. Her wiles and experience kept her cautious. Knowing she was following, the Preacher kept her prepared for anything.

"Lo? Anyone about?" Ada called into the dark maw of the dirt hill. "Hey there? Y'all around?"

The large, simple door was ajar and hung on leather hinges. Ada, drawing the hammer back on her rifle, crossed the threshold. Her worn boots slid across the dusty ground and her footing stayed stable.

Pupils dilated from the sun. It took a moment for Ada's eyes to adjust to the windowless dimness of the interior. The acrid smell of gunpowder filled her nostrils, along with the smell of old earth and decay. Kerosene lanterns hung from posts around the room and gave off a bare minimum of light that created as many dark shadows as areas they illuminated.

The room Ada found herself in was large and cluttered with debris. Shadows were layered everywhere among countless crates, boxes, and bric-à-brac. Natural light struggled to leak in through the south-facing door behind her. The room was dry, yet built deep into the ground. Ada was amazed as she took in the space quickly.

"Wish we could use sumthin' like this in the swamp. We'd drown, though," Ada mumbled to herself.

Ada wove slowly through the maze of merchandise while staying low. The two bullet wounds she received in the Dakota Territory, not fully healed yet no longer bleeding, aggravated her and would not allow her to take the position as deeply as she desired. As she crept through the flotsam and jetsam, she heard moans of pain.

A man shouted from behind the small bar, "Witch! Watch watcha yer doin!"

Ada leaned over the counter and saw a grizzled man down on the floor. Perched next to the yelling man, Ada saw a native woman who appeared to be wrapping bandages around the man's bloody hand.

"Damnit woman, yer makin' it worse." The old man cursed and pressed his eyes closed. His face was red with pain and covered in deep wrinkles.

The woman bandaging him did not respond and instead focused on working quickly and quietly, her dark fingers moving diligently.

Ada uncocked her rifle and cleared her throat before speaking up, "Hey, y'all."

The man looked up in alarm, his eyes popping open. "What? Who're you?" He squinted at her in suspicion. His good hand darted around the floor near him, trying to find purchase on the knife on the floor less than a foot from him.

Ada narrowed her eyes. "Jist ridin' through, lookin' fer trade," Ada stated. She looked around, then added, "Supplies are low." Ada's lips were tight as she returned the man's suspicious gaze. "Did ah jist miss 'em?"

The quiet woman looked up at Ada and nodded.

"Yeah," the man's eyes darkened as he sighed a great breath and sagged to the floor. "You just missed me getting robbed by a big burly sonofabitch," he cursed.

"Rode west?" Ada asked, as her thoughts turned to the Preacher.

"No shit," the man's temper was up and he spoke abruptly. "He got a gang yonder," he gestured with his good hand in the general direction the rider had departed. "Rode in here, shot my hand, and cleaned me out." He cursed, "Bastards, all of 'em." The wounded man tried to spit, but failed and only sputtered.

The native women helped the man stand and shook her head.

Ada pursed her lips. "What of the law?" she asked.

The man rolled his eyes and spoke condescendingly to Ada, "Ain't no law here." Then he asked in exasperation, "Do you see a town out here?" Holding himself upright on the bar using his good hand, he continued, "This here is just a simple trading post for travelers. Ain't nuthin' else out here for many miles around."

Considering that this would be the last opportunity to restock, Ada thought over her valuables. Ada had little money and few skins left to trade since passing the Wilson farm, and ever since entering into these long rolling hills, she had seen fewer deer. All she had field dressed of note were rabbits.

"Can't eat hides," Ada grumbled as she offered what she had to the man for trade.

The man shook his head. "Got no need for skins. Plenty of that around." He gestured to the crates stacked halfway to the ceiling toward the back of the post. Ada chewed her lip for a moment, knowing she needed supplies in the coming weeks.

"There a bounty on 'em?" Ada bit her jaw and stole herself for what was coming next.

The old man shook his head. "Nah, none that I know of," he paused, "yet. They are criminals of disrepute and harass all God's creatures at every turn."

Ada took a moment to consider what the man was saying. Ada scanned the wrapped hand of the trader and deduced that it wasn't anything to worry over.

Bandaging done, the woman stepped toward Ada and spoke for the first time. "You kill, I pay."

The man looked stricken and grumbled, "Who pays?" The old trader shifted his weight to a nearby stool with an audible sigh. The old stool beneath him creaked dangerously under his weight.

Ada saw a familiar opportunity. "Ah don't need money, jist supplies."

The man did not immediately respond, his eyes lingering on his wounded hand.

The woman nodded curtly.

Mulling over the offer without taking his eyes from his bandaging, the man said, "Well, it don't cost me nothing if you die, so." He shrugged his acceptance and held out his dirty, unharmed hand. "James," he said.

The bold woman from Louisiana accepted his hand. "Ada."

She walked out of the trading post briskly and, with momentum, limping a little less, and over to her horse. She led the large red roan away from the trading post by his bridle.

"Got us a bit of a distraction, boy. We ain't gonna make it down to New Mexico with what's on us." She patted the old leather bags draping the roan's back that lay flat and nearly empty. Ada sighed deeply as she stepped into her stirrup and swung her leg over the cantle. "Hope Athena's shitty Spencer don't break," she said as she slid the rifle into the scabbard.

She gave a moment of thought to the woman who had sold her the rifle and a broken-down nag when she hunted the

Preacher up north. Ada had been desperate and Athena had taken full advantage of that fact. She hoped Athena was cold in the ground.

Ada pulled at the reins and turned her horse toward the setting sun, the same direction in which the man that had ridden away earlier. She rode her roan at a trot as Ada considered the landscape with eyes narrow and on the lookout for danger.

Ada rode the red roan in a westward direction for almost an hour. The ride took her to a small barranca cut into the earth that was surrounded by pocked outcroppings of stone.

The sound of horses echoed from inside the canyon and Ada also picked up the sound of a man yelling, "Settle down, ya damn nag."

Holding the horn, Ada stepped down from her horse and led him over to a small grove of trees. Once there, she tied him to a hackberry and drew the Spencer rifle from its scabbard. Taking slow and deliberate steps, she made her way into the canyon, both alert and watchful for the man who had shouted.

Her body fought against her as Ada crept through the brush. Her muscles were sore and stiff, and she drove them relentlessly. Ada took a deep breath and pushed through the wall of discomfort that tried to restrict her from completing her task. After forty yards of creeping through stone and brush, Ada heard more voices.

"Damn, McLane, you shot him in the hand. What the hell?" A man's voice carried on the wind.

Another man whined, "That old dirtbag, he should'a been more careful."

A third man spoke up, "You two are sorry sacks of shit. You bring shame upon the McLane name."

Ada thought for a moment, but the name was not one she knew.

The third man continued, "The three of us ain't no account of a gang without any *big scores*."
Ada was only able to pull out a few louder parts of the conversation. The rest of the grumbling was lost on her.

She waited, poised upon a small flat outcropping of stone with her rifle at the ready. Almost an hour passed without incident as she waited for an opportunity to move in. She had only heard three men talking and wanted to make that there were only three members of the gang.

The sky was starting to turn colors by the time she stepped out with rifle cocked and aimed.

"What the hell?" one of the men yelled in surprise when he realized Ada had positioned herself so she could cover all three targets with a minimal amount of movement.

"Don't do nuthin' stupid," she growled in a low and threatening voice. Her body was still and her voice calm, but her eyes were alight with fire. "Ah'm jist here to get back what was took."

The men each sat frozen and stupefied.

A moment passed as Ada scrutinized the three. "Y'all jist kids," she said, realizing how young they were. Ada looked them over and perceived little threat to herself from the cowardly bunch. Not a man had twitched, nor had they looked for a weapon.

One of the young men spoke up. "We ain't no chicken shit kids, you backshoot'n us."

A smirk creased Ada's face. "Alright, just throw yer guns thata way," she gestured with the business end of the Spencer to the brush nearby. Ada positioned herself so that all three men were covered by her barrel and all three men knew it. Her side turned to them. She signaled again with the barrel and cocked an eyebrow.

One at a time, the men threw their guns into the brush.

Ada took a slow breath. "Ah appreciate y'all bein' so sociable. Hand over that gold piece what ya took from that trader's place."

The men looked at each other and shifted their weight nervously.

The young man who had spoken first cleared his throat and said, "Well," he looked about sheepishly, "we ain't got nothin' like that."

Ada squinted at him. "Don't play, boy," she said while gesturing again with the rifle.

Another of the young men spoke up, "It-it, it was Uncle James." He spoke nervously, and the other two cast dark eyes upon him.

"Donnie, shut up," an elbow shot out from the third boy and hit the one he called Donnie in the side.

Ada tilted her head. "Uncle James? What in the hell is goin' on here?" Her patience was fading fast and the trio heard the agitation in her voice.

Ada cocked her hammer and pressed her lips into a thin white line. "Names, now," she commanded them coldly and with a steely gaze.

"I'm Donnie McLane, these here are my brothers," the first to speak up said as he gestured with his head toward the others.

"I'm Charlie," said the one who had been arguing with Donnie. Charlie kicked his boot into the last brother. "And this sour thing is George," the young man stated.

George tipped his hat to Ada, but kept his eyes on the ground.

Ada clenched her jaw and looked with wary eyes upon the men as she considered the situation. "So, *Uncle James*, huh?"

Donnie nodded and looked at his shredded boot toes.

Ada thumbed the hammer on the rifle. "Why?" She asked, "What fer?" Ada stood quiet to let the McLanes talk.

Charlie spoke up, "We was working for him. We pretend to rob him and hope somebody with means comes this a way." He hung his head low.

Ada chuckled dryly, "How's that workin fer ya?" She shook her head and sucked at her teeth.

"We got the drop on one last week," George spoke. "We didn't kill nobody, just took his valuables."

Ada spat, "Jist thieve'n, huh?"

The shoulders of each of the men sagged, and each had shame written across their faces.

"Damnit, git tied." Ada threw some rope at the men that she had hung on her shoulder. She realized they were probably teens as she watched them.

They grumbled and cursed under their breath as they complied while faced with the barrel of Ada's gun.

The walk back was slow, the pace set by the bound men. Ada followed on the roan and shook her head from time to time in disgust. It was dark by the time they arrived at the trading post.

Ada yelled out to the proprietor, "James, I got yer bounty!"

Sounds of shuffling and boxes falling over came from the building. James peeked out of the door a moment later and saw his three nephews.

"Oh, shit," he muttered. He turned his head, looking left, and came eye to eye with the barrel of Ada's Spencer.

She cocked the rifle and held it leveled at his head. "Yea, ya done stepped in it, James."

The man came slowly out of the building with his hands raised. He cursed at the three tied up after catching them with his eye. "You no account worthless sacks of shit!"

Each of the tied were red-faced with indignation and embarrassment.

Donnie spoke back, "She snuck up on us because ya didn't signal!" James rolled his eyes and held up his bandaged hand.

"You three are worthless! My hand took a slug!"

Donnie was about to defend himself when James pulled out his six-shooter and spun on Ada.

She pulled the trigger, but her Spencer jammed.

Ada cursed in surprise and frustration. Light blasted out of the darkness as a bullet grazed Ada. She threw herself from her saddle and rolled. Before more lead could be flung her way, she leapt and swung her rifle like a club.

The stock of Ada's gun took James in the jaw and Ada saw his eyes roll.

As James stumbled back, George kicked out at him, tripping

James and sending him tumbling to the ground. James dropped one knee to the dirt and caught himself with his free hand and, still armed, he lifted the gun with a shaky grip.

A shot rang out from the building to Ada's right.

James dropped his gun, his shirt blossoming in a flower of red.

Ada turned and saw the native woman standing with the gun in her hand, still smoking.

George, still tied to Donnie and Charlie, stumbled over to her while pulling his brothers along.

The woman, as if suddenly coming to her senses, dropped the weapon to the ground like it was a snake.

Donnie and Charlie looked in shock at their dead uncle James, their brother George, and the woman.

"Naw hold on folks." Ada cocked the rifle. "This here ain't gonna misfire again." Ada nodded to the rifle.

George jumped in front of the dark woman and pulled his stumbling brothers along with him. "Stop, she had to do it!"

Ada saw the looks of confusion on the other two faces and calculated her next move.

George's hands, still bound, were held out in front of him as he talked. "This is Tadita of the Ponca. I love her," Charlie squawked.

Tadita looked at the two other brothers and then at the body of James, "I am sorry. He was bad. Hurt me."

A bright moon was rising and Ada could see the black eye, earlier hidden by hair and darkness as Tadita stepped outside of the trading post.

"I am for George only," she stated surely.

George stood tall and proud. "We are promised to each other by her people."

Ada uncocked her rifle and shifted her weight. "Hold on now," she spoke to Tadita. "Ya told me ya'd pay me to kill," Ada gestured to the tied men.

"Yes," Tadita responded nodding tightly. "Kill him." She pointed at the dead man.

Ada rocked on her heels for a moment, removed her hat, and wiped her brow with the back of her hand.

George turned to Ada and said, "Can you untie us now?"

Ada stood still for a moment, thinking over the situation, doffed her hat, and then nodded. "Y'all a damn mess," Ada said as she gestured to Tadita.

At the gesture, Tadita moved to untie her lover and his brothers while Ada walked over to the sloping earth and took a seat while keeping the rifle at her side.

The three brothers commenced to arguing as soon as they were freed. Meanwhile, Tadita walked over and sat down on the grass by Ada.

"Thank you," Tadita said softly.

Ada nodded with pursed lips and tilted her head while watching the men go at each other. "It's alright. Damn mess this is, though."

Tadita nodded and looked at her feet.

"Am I hanging?" Tadita asked quietly.

Ada looked toward the darkness and the wilds beyond the horizon. "Nah, ain't no law here seems." Ada stood and gestured to James's body laying on the hard-packed earth. "Ya fellas might want to have a quick funeral fer yer bottom feedin' uncle."

Ada scooped up the dead man's gun. Not a single person moved to stop her as she holstered it in one of the empty leathers at her hip and sighed. "Feels alright," she grumbled while gauging the weight. She drew the gun quickly and then rolled the cylinder.

The three young men watched Ada quietly before they looked at each other.

"Shovels are inside," said George.

"How much?" asked Tadita.

Ada shook her head before she looked at Tadita with her brow furrowed. "Jist supplies, no coin."

The dark woman nodded and went inside the trading post hill.

Light flickered on from several oil lamps as Tadita lit the few lanterns in the structure. She moved gracefully around the room for a short amount of time while rummaging around in and collecting goods.

When she emerged again, Tadita had a few sacks that she handed to Ada. "Full and," she paused while looking Ada in the eyes, "thank you."

Ada watched Tadita as she went back into the structure with eyes starting to well with tears.

The three brothers finished with the burial just as the sun came up. They met Ada, dirty and exhausted, as she was loading her goods on the roan.

"That's a good strong rope, ma'am," Donnie noted of the rope Ada had previously tied the trio with. He grinned a bit and slapped the dirt off of himself.

Ada shook her head, sighed, and gave them a disgusted look. She held out her hand to Tadita who had also come outside again. "Ya got this?" Ada said, while gesturing to the three young men.

The Ponca woman nodded. "I'm running this place now," she said while indicating to the trading post.

"Well," Ada gestured to the fresh mound of dirt piled the side of the building. "Do better than that there fella."

"What's your name?" Charlie pipped up.
"Ada," she said as she turned away. "Ada Picou." She donned the hat that Tadita had given her from the post's goods. It was unbleached, had no marbling, and suited her.

Ada pivoted and stepped her boot into the roan's stirrup. She pushed up into the saddle, swinging her bad leg over the cantle. Once seated and with reins in hand, Ada threw a wave to Tadita who was leaning against the door jamb.

The roan rode southerly and to the west. All the while Ada kept her eyes peeled for signs of New Mexico, and the Preacher she knew was ahead of her.

CHAPTER THREE

Standing beside a scraggly old tree, Ada peeled off a layer of her coarse clothing and tucked it into her bedroll. Her eyes took in the lone tree on the grassy hill. Gray bark that was brittle and thick scattered the ground at her feet.

"Ya look like a moccasin that's growin' in the spring." She gave the tree another look before pulling her hat from a cracked branch. "'cept ya ain't growin' none no more." She slid her callused hand over the rough bark and directed her gaze south.

The air grew warmer as Ada and the roan traveled. Animals began showing more of themselves on the far sides of the lightly worn road, making it easier to find small game for Ada's growing collection. The meat she kept in the bags of salt. She also kept a sharp eye out for water. Her roan was needing more water as they entered into the drier climate.

Ada had picked up a second six-shooter and a few cases of shells from Tadita and George. On the first night away from the trading post, Ada resumed her old habits. The routines of the evening brought her comfort and settled her nerves as she hunted the Preacher.

She took the saddle and girth off of the roan and set them near where she would rest for the night and mused, "Ya sweatin' more." In the new rucksack, she also found a brush and hoof pick.

The roan stood still and swished his tail, glad to be brushed. There was a good deal of hair that came out with each swipe over the horse's hardy body.

"Lotta that winter coats comin' out," Ada spoke calmly and kindly to the large animal. Brushing complete, she braced his leg between her knees and set herself to picking at his hooves. "Ain't so bad," she said to herself. He had been on frozen ground for a season and she was satisfied with the state his hooves were in when she had expected them to be in far worse shape.

Going through these motions calmed both the horse and Ada. After the roan was brushed and hobbled for the night, Ada basked in the amber glow of the mesquite fire. The flames were small at first, and Ada kept them going by placing dried buffalo chips in the shallow dugout she'd made.

"Glad I been pickin' them up," Ada commented as she watched the flames burn slowly through the dried waste.

Ada sat on her heels and set herself to roasting a pheasant on a large knife. She turned the meet with care and held the bird just above the flames. Fat that dripped from the meat sizzled in the small fire. The bird cooked slowly, and she savored the smell as the aroma filled her nostrils. A gentle and warm breeze from the south slid by her and instilled Ada with a comfortable feeling that reminded her of home.

Pheasant finished, Ada next set the coffee to boil as she ate.

"Ahm almost feelin' normal," Ada stated to the fire, or the

horse, or herself, as she slowly enjoyed the food and drink.

It had been a long time since Ada allowed herself such comforts. When she didn't move about too much, she could ignore the pain in her leg. Even the burn on her tongue from the too-hot coffee was a nice bit of normal.

After eating the game and drinking the coffee, Ada's thoughts wandered to the oil Tadita had given her for her saddle and boots, something she was eager to put to good use.

Ada rubbed oil into all of her leather goods and worked the oil into her worn boots last. "They ain't gonna last much longer," she noted, while eyeing the thin soles and thinner toes.

The saddle, one of Ada's most prized possessions, shone in the fire's umber, cinder-crossed glow. Even in the low-flickering flames, the craftsmanship stood out. Colors of brown, tan, and black all held together with metal rivets and thick stitching, Ada couldn't help but shake her head in amazement at what could be made from hides in the hands of a true craftsman.

Without a moon looking down upon the prairies, the darkness soon covered everything around Ada in a deep, dark velvet. Only the area near the fire remained visible as the night waxed on. Knowing she was far behind the Preacher put Ada at partial ease that night. Ada had little concern that the fire might attract any unwanted company, as she had taken precautions to keep it low to the ground and small in the shallow pit that she had dug out and was blocked from view by the dirt she piled on its south side.

About an hour later and Ada had rubbed oil into her saddle,

the outside of the bags, her belts, holsters, rifle scabbard, knife sheaths, boots, and anything else she could find.

"Restless," she muttered. Ada then spotted the two guns she'd gained from the trading post.

"Well, damn," she mumbled. "Don't nobody care fer nothin' no more?" She turned the guns in her hand and inspected them for wear and damage. The oil she had been given would help a little, but it would not work miracles. "Better than nothin', ah suppose."

It was deep into the night by the time Ada was finished burning through her tasks. Alone and in the dark, she settled in and set herself to sleep. With bedroll spread out, boots to one side and with guns on the other, she gave one last look to her saddle and other belongings.

She nodded. Everything was just as it should be.

As she closed her eyes, lids finally heavy with fatigue, Ada caught a flash of light far to the south. She propped herself up on an elbow just as the sound of a gunshot reached her ears.

Ada squinted into the darkness and mumbled, "far, too far to worry over it," and lay back down with her shoulders parallel to the ground. "South," she muttered as her mind drifted, pricked by needling anxiety, into a poor and fitful sleep.

Dawn eventually broke over the horizon and crept its way across the rolling plains.

Ada greeted the emerging gray with weary muscles and a foggy head. Body stiff and sore from the hard earth and troubled sleep, she dug through her pack for her water skin. She huffed, "Mornin's gettin' earlier, boy."

Ada's joints popped and cracked as she packed up her bedroll and tied it behind the saddle. She absently rubbed at the wound on her leg as she looked south, her lips down-turned in a tight and grim look. There was a nagging worry in her belly that left her with no appetite for breakfast.

Guns holstered, loaded, and cleaned, Ada rode high in the saddle with her toes up and her back straight. Even the roan acted eager and trotted along with his steps quick and his ears perked. The sun sat upon Ada's right and warmed her, softening her sore spots. As she rode south, she spied vultures in the sky ahead of her.

"Ah reckon that's 'bout where that gunfire was," Ada spoke to the horse and worried her lip. She was headed in a southerly direction and her curiosity convinced her that a slight detour wouldn't cause harm to her journey. She soon noted a dark mass in the distance and she pressed the roan onward and straight for it.

As Ada rode closer the scene before her unfolded and she was able to surmise more of what'd happened the previous night.

There was an overturned wagon and the mules that had pulled it were all shot dead. Her sharp eyes took in the blood-splatted stones. She drew her gun and held it poised in her hand, at the ready for any trouble that might remain among the ruins.

Ada's eyes caught the glint of light reflected off the shells scattered about and, closing in, she came upon two bodies.

The duo lay but a few feet from the wagon. Seated high in the saddle, she could see they were that of a man and a woman. Neither person moved as they splayed themselves prone and with limbs askew.

Without peeling her eyes from her surroundings, Ada stepped slowly and carefully out of the saddle. Ada gave a slight pat to the roan's haunch and had him trot off. The only sounds Ada heard were of the roan and the wagon's torn canvas snapping in the breeze.

Keeping low to the ground and with her gun cocked, she made her way over to the bodies. "Maybe these folks crossed sacred ground or happened upon an Apache huntin' party," Ada surmised, as she surveyed the site.

However, she spotted neither arrows nor tracks to match such a party. There was only one set, and the familiarity of them unnerved her.

Ada's face tightened and her forehead creased pensively in concern over a host of misgivings.

Ada crept over to the man and tentatively placed her hand on his shoulder. The man's body was heavy and stiff as she turned him over.

The blood drained from Ada's face.

Ada was unsurprised to find that the man had been shot, but his slit throat shocked her. Images of her brother, mother, and father flooded her mind as she shot bolt upright and rocked on her heels.

Ada's gasps for breath were punctuated with her repeated mumbles of "No, no, no—!

The world spun around Ada. It was him, the Preacher. The man with the piercing blue eyes. The man she hunted in the Dakota Territory and now followed back to New Mexico had been so close.

Ada's thigh throbbed with memory and she fought to compose herself as she sucked in air through the gaps in her clenched teeth. "God damn sonofabitch—!" Ada bit back bile and, with a tight, thin lip, walked over to inspect the woman's corpse next. Ada steeled herself before turning over the body, knowing what she would likely see.

Just as the man had been, the woman gunned down and her throat slit.

Ada surmised from the amount of blood that they had been shot first and then cut later. It was a gruesome scene that sent Ada into frantic thought:

This was done for her. That Preacher had intended for her to find this, and he knew how close she was. The similarities were too close. Ada these people were left for her to find. As she realized this, she was glad she'd skipped breakfast that morning.

Ada's heart raced, sweat rolled off of her brow, and her hands shook. As she struggled to fight the memories of finding Arden, Mary, and Joel just like this all those years ago.

Preoccupied as she was, Ada almost missed a sound that came from under the wagon.

"Oh, shit," Ada said as she spun around with guns drawn and ready to shoot the Preacher if he emerged.

A small shadow moved in the shade under the upturned wagon. It was too close to the ground and small to belong to the Preacher, Ada realized.

"Maybe its jist a dog," Ada hoped in a low whisper. The six-shooters still steady in her hand, Ada's reflexes to danger refused to allow her nerves to settle. Her hands were no longer shaking and the pain in her leg was far from her mind.

The shadow scurried about, but nothing emerged from under the wagon.

"Come on nah," she spoke softly. She kept the fear from her voice as best she could while trying to coax out whatever was hiding from her. She remembered the jerk in her pack and grumbled, "Maybe a little meat'll tempt it?"

Ada clicked to the roan, and he trotted back to her side. As Ada turned to her horse, she heard another small sound.

"Please don't hurt me."

Ada froze, her eyes wide in shock. The guns almost fell from her hands as, with feet rooted in the ground, she turned slowly and with great effort. Her searching eyes fell upon something even more unexpected crawling out of the remains of the wagon.

A young girl, covered in filth, staggered to her feet and met Ada's gaze.

CHAPTER FOUR

Both Colt pistols slid effortlessly into the leathers on Ada's belt. She forgot to speak for a moment and only slightly shook her head in stunned silence.

"Ah ain't," Ada's voice eventually came. It bubbled up from her gut and was coarse and deep. There was a raw severity in her tone that spoke of her life of desperation.

Ada eyed the girl and noted the blood and filth darkening the young girl's clothes.

Ada nodded and asked, "ya hurt?"

The girl shook her brown curls slowly as she walked toward Ada, stepping past the dead adults without looking at them. Hazel eyes kissed with gold flecks bore into Ada.

"Who're ya?" Ada asked, not being able to think of anything else to inquire about due to how her mind was scattered.

This had all been a calling card of the Preacher. He had left this marker of death for her to find. There were so many similarities between this and her own loss.

Ada stood pale-faced and waiting for, but not expecting, the girl to answer. Ada knew shock and what it would do to a person.

The girl walked up to Ada and gazed up at her with red and puffy eyes. She spoke in barely a whisper when she said, "My name is Adelle." The small thing swallowed hard and then fell to the ground unconscious.

Ada squatted down and checked the girl over for wounds. Finding none, Ada lifted her small frame and carried the child toward the roan.

Once the trio was fifty yards further from the carnage, Ada made a small fire and staked the roan. She'd set the unconscious Adelle on the opened bedroll and, while the child rested set herself to burying the man and woman on a small hill she found near the overturned wagon.

Through her own tight chest Ada murmured, "Must be tha' girl's ma and pa."

Ada took a shovel from the wagon and dug a shallow grave. She cursed the Preacher with every heaving breath as she filled the hole with the two dead. She was shaken to her core and, after finishing, sat for a moment to collect herself. Wiping her brow with her arm and with hat in hand, she surveyed the scene with fresh eyes.

"Damn him to Hell." Ada cursed and spat and worried if Hell was enough.

Ada set her eyes on the dirt on her hands and under her nails. Her hands again shook and her leg burned. She tapped the flask in her pocket, her father's flask. It had been refilled at the trading post, and now Ada took a generous pull on the coffin varnish. The rye burned as it went down. It settled her, and softened her fears. Her eyes drifted to the girl.

"Still asleep, looks like, poor heart," she said in a low and kindly voice. Ada shook her head and looked at the sky. "Lord, make me yer weapon. Ah don't ask fer nothin' else, jist let me end him." Ada fidgeted, shifted her weight, and then added, "Amen."

Ada stood, her joints once again creaking, and walked over to the horse and the girl. Adelle's eyes were open now, and the girl stared up at the sky with a distant gaze.

"They are my parents."

Ada nodded, noticing for the first time the girl's foreign accent.

Calmly the young girl added, "He has my brother."

Ada's boots crunched against the gravel and she turned her eyes to Adelle, saying incredulously, "What you sayin' girl?"

"He said you would help," Adelle stated. Tears flowed out of her eyes and cut through the dirt on the girl's dusty face.

"Dear God," Ada breathed out as a new fear settled into her chest. She threw her eyes to the southern horizon before Ada clenched her jaw and set a steely look upon the girl.

Adelle looked stricken, flinched, and for a moment panicked. She raised herself on her elbows and kicked away from Ada.

"Ah ain't gonna do ya nuthin," Ada said as she squatted down to the girl's level and put her hands up. Ada was calm when she spoke, her voice firm when she said, "Ah jist wanna help ya."

Ada could feel the girl's assessing scrutiny upon her. After a moment passed, a quiet nod was all Adelle could muster.

"Can ah set ya on my horse?" Ada asked.

Adelle nodded, again looking dazed and distant.

Ada lifted Adelle easily. "Y'all been traveling for a spell seems."

The red roan stood still and allowed Ada to place the girl in the saddle.

"Hold here a minute," Ada said as she put the girl's hands on the leather-wrapped horn. Ada worried her lip and looked back to the shared grave.

"You'll pray for them, won't you?" Adelle asked.

Ada's eyebrows tightened and her eyes darkened. "Yeah."

Ada could smell the kerosene spilled in the wagon that ruined everything inside. Limping slightly, she made her way over to the wreckage, struck a match, and then set the wagon on fire. "These people suffered 'nough. Ain't no need to draw the attention of bandits or robbers to this here grave," she grumbled.

Showdown

Ada stood in silence by the mound of fresh dirt as the wagon went up in a blaze.

The prayers she whispered were for the little girl and her brother. She once more asked God to not judge her harshly for killing the man she hunted. The fire highlighted her features and cast a long shadow containing much of Ada's rage. "Amen," she spoke tightly as fury shook her frame.
Once the ruined cart and all its contents were all but completely reduced to ashes, Ada pivoted on her heel and locked eyes with Adelle who was still sitting upon the roan.

Ada wondered how such things could happen as she walked back to the horse.

"Is my brother going to die?" Adelle asked in a low, pleading voice as Ada approached.

Ada gnashed her teeth and looked over the terrain. "We'll git him back." Then she added, "He'll be alright." She awkwardly patted the girl's shoulder and frowned at the girl's soft, dirty locks.

Adelle sat trembling in the saddle and leaned back into Ada. After walking the roan past the decreasing flames and up to the grave, they stopped.

"Please, Lord," Ada whispered one last time.

Adelle's small hands clutched the horn, her tiny knuckles white.

CHAPTER FIVE

As they rode off after the Preacher's trail, Ada picked up on the sound of Adelle mumbling something in a quiet voice. For a moment Ada thought it must be the shock of everything catching up to the girl, but as Ada listened, it became clear that the little girl was praying. There was not much that Ada could make out, yet there was something familiar about the sound.

"Ya talkin' French?" Ada asked with surprise in her voice. She had not heard words like these in years.

Adelle nodded solemnly. "I am French."

"Ya don't sound French, though." She thought for a second and added, "Least, ya don't sound like any Frenchies ah know."

Adelle shifted upright and stiffened. "You know people from France?"

Ada shook her head. "Nah. Not from France, but they're French."

The girl sat in front of Ada and thought quietly to herself.

Looking down, Ada could only see the crown of the girl's head and not her expression.

The two rode in silence for the remainder of the day.

At dusk, Ada set up a small camp. She banked the small fire in a shallow pit, as she had always done ever since she became aware that the Preacher was leading her south.

Adelle watched with a focused gaze as Ada rubbed the roan down and picked his hooves. She watched everything Ada did with great interest, even when Ada merely boiled water for coffee and rolled out the bedding.

Once she was finished caring for the horse, Ada set herself to preparing supper using a snake she'd killed earlier in the day.

"Not the best meat, but I want the supplies to last," Ada commented as she looked to the packs and worried about their journey considering there were now two mouths to feed.

Adelle frowned at the idea of eating the serpent.

The speckled horse was jittery when Ada retrieved the snake from a saddle bag near where the roan was tied up.

"Don't ya worry none boy," Ada said, while throwing the roan a glance. "He ain't gonna do ya nuthin." Ada used one of her many knives to slice off the snake's head. She then rolled the skin back and said, "like takin' off a sock.". it was something she recalled her father saying when she was young.

Ada cooked the greasy meat in a small skillet Ada had received from George, and the small meal was soon served.

"It's chewy," Adelle observed distastefully.

"Its food," Ada responded. Ada put a piece from the pan too quickly into her mouth.

"*Fils-putain!*" Ada cursed and spit the meat back into her hand. She blew on the small scrap of meat to help it cool.

Maybe it was the trauma of the past few months trapped in the snowy wastes of the Dakota Territory. Maybe it was being around Adelle. It was the first French Ada had uttered in years.

Adelle turned red, but looked unsure of what to make of what had just happened.

Ada quickly turned a shade of pink herself. "Sounds different in French. Don't it?" Ada shrugged off the tension.

Adelle peered at Ada. "Are you French?"

Ada nodded. "My people are from Louisiana." She thought for a moment and looked into the fire. "Ah reckon they came from Canada a long time ago, not sure 'bout that though." Ada looked at the ground and squinted. "My Mere and Pere spoke French. Ma and Pa didn't speak much of it, though. Jist a bit now and then."

Adelle looked at Ada quizzically. "Where is Louisiana? Is it near Paris?"

Ada shook her head in confusion. "Nah, it's a thousand miles that way." She pointed over her shoulder to the southeast.

Adelle did not look away from the fire, but spoke sadly and with a puzzled expression, "I never saw Paris. We were on the boat and I was sick after."

Ada matched Adelle's curious look. "Louisiana ain't in France," she explained. "It's on the Mississippi River, in the United States of America," Ada said.

"But," Adelle's lips drew tight, "you said you were French. Are you a liar? "You don't sound like mama and papa," the girl added skeptically.

"Ah. ain't. lyin." Ada emphasized each word as she felt her ire rise. "Ah've lived all over, but my people's French at the Atchafalya."

Adelle shook her head. "You are American, yes? You speak confusing English, but yes? You are, in fact, American."

Red crawled up Ada's neck to her face. "Yeah, ah'm American. My pa fought for us in war." Ada added, "Ah'm also French, ah speak it too."

Ada said a few curse words in her French and again the girl blushed. Ada finished brewing coffee and tossed the dregs into the crackling flames. The coffee was sour, and she frowned.

"Maybe that damn snake ruined my taste." She wiped her cup and the skillet down. "We gotta put this out." Ada looked at Adelle and, still with mild annoyance in her tone, said, "You done girl?"

Adelle responded with a nervous nod.

After smothering the fire, the two crawled together into the bedroll.

"I'm sorry Miss Ada," the young girl spoke gravely.

Ada sighed, her anger long vanished. "It ain't nuthin. Jist need to turn is all."

Adelle curled up into Ada's arms, seeking warmth. "Will we get Henri back?"

Ada nodded in the darkness. "Yea, we'll git him back."

Despite her need to rest and keep prepared for the troubles surely lying in wait ahead, Ada stayed up most of the night. She considered her situation, the plight of the young girl swaddled in her blanket, and the boy she prayed she'd find alive.
As Adelle drifted off, she whispered quietly, "My mama called me Peachie."

Ada silently nodded. She watched the stars glinting overhead as a quiet tear slid down the girl's face in the cool darkness.

CHAPTER SIX

"Ya come from a city?" Ada asked Peachie one day after observing the girl's refined way of carrying herself during their travels.

The girl nodded. "Sort of. I'm from a town not far outside of Paris."

"Yer daddy hunted?"

"Yes, he was a good shot."

Ada cocked an eyebrow. "Was he now?" Ada sized up the girl with fresh perspective. "How about you?"

"My mama said I was not allowed." Peachie shook her head. "Only Henri. When he gets older."

Ada shrugged and looked off to the distant horizon. "Alright then. Ya gotta learn to shoot."

Peachie watched Ada, sensing a change in the woman's bearing.

Ada and Peachie eventually stopped to make camp when the sun had just started to fall below the horizon. The fire was low, and the coffee was hot. Peachie set the bedroll out, as was her usual task each day. Meanwhile, Ada pulled the Spencer from the leather scabbard on the horse and tossed it to Peachie.

The young girl caught it awkwardly. She threw Ada a confused look and held the gun as though it were a viperous kin of the snake she'd been forced to consume days prior.

"Here ya are." Ada gestured to the gun and then casually pointed to a cottonwood tree twenty-five yards off. "Can ya hit that?" Ada tilted her head to the target.

Peachie pressed her lips together into a tight line and squinted at the tree. "Is the gun loaded?"

Ada walked over with a smile on her face and showed Peachie the bullets in the stock.

Peachie, gun in hand, walked a few feet away. She laid on the dirt and braced the stock of the gun against her shoulder. She aimed for a moment before she fired, popping a good chunk of bark off the tree.

Ada whistled and adjusted her hat as dry dust blew away in the breeze. "Damn girl, ya ain't bad."

Peachie stood and looked at the ground as she shyly chewed her lip. "Thanks."

"There's more to ah gun than shootin'." Ada said as she took the Spencer back.

That night, she taught Peachie the names for each of the parts of the Spencer and how to go about cleaning it.

"What if we don't have gun oil," Peachie asked.

Ada gestured to the fire. "Tallow. "We clean up some animal fat good and let it set. Works well in a pinch."

Peachie listened intently and repeated back everything Ada said.

"Yer ah smart one, huh?" Ada observed.

"I know my letters and numbers," Peachie stated proudly.

"Not bad kid, not bad at all," Ada chuckled.

Over the next few days, whenever Ada stopped the roan she let Peachie hunt.

"Huntin' is different than shootin'. Ya sort of got to think like an animal. Ya gotta leave the person ya are behind," Ada explained as best she could.

Peachie observed Ada with a look of confusion on her face.

"Ya can't rightly run somethin' down on a horse or nuthin' and no animal is jist waitin' around to get itself shot," Ada went on. "Huntin' is slow, and it takes all ya got." Ada chewed her lip in frustration. "Ah ain't no good at teachin' this. Jist listen, watch, smell, and feel fer them." Ada plopped hard on the ground with her knees turned up. Peachie had pulled her usually wild hair back into a swinging braid that swayed with her every move. "Ya jist have to watch me fer a spell and see."

The diligent Peachie nodded with a tight bob of her head.

On this particular occasion, Ada taught Peachie to track small game by the scat and prints various creatures left behind.

"Ya can tell what yer after when ya at this here scat."

Peachie turned her nose up as Ada poked some feces with a stick.

"Whoa naw, don't get too prim 'bout this. It'll save ya from huntin' somethin' ya can't manage." Ada could tell that, despite her discomfort, Peachie was trying to understand. "Plus, scat'll tell ya how nearby an animal is by how dried up its shit is."

Ada even showed Peachie how to bring down rabbits and pheasants by "always keeping the iron on 'em" as Ada liked to preach.. The Spencer had a true aim and only occasionally misfired. While hunting in a gully, Ada and Peachie spotted turkey. "Aim a little high here and when ya pull the trigger breathe out."

Peachie did as she was told, and that night they plucked and ate a fresh tom turkey.

"Ya done real well. Ah reckon after a few years ya might manage on yer own." Ada patted the girl on the shoulder.

Peachie scrunched her brow. "I don't want to live with Henri out here!" She gestured to the great expanse around them. "We are going back to France as soon as I find him."

"Why? What ya got there?"

Peachie looked helplessly around. "Nothing. Same as here." Tears welled in the girl's eyes.

Ada nodded and looked at the horizon with a sorrowful expression. "Alright Peachie, alright." She scratched at her neck nervously and suddenly regretted asking.

Full on turkey, but still keeping an eye on the darkness, the two sat in an awkward silence. Peachie lost herself staring into the small dying flames, her steady gaze interrupted only when Ada stood and walked over to the saddle where she again drew the Spencer from the scabbard.

"Ya earned it." Ada strode over to where Peachie sat on the ground with her hands wrapped around her knees and extended the rifle to Peachie.

Ada could see Peachie weighing and measuring the gift, if gift it was, with her eyes for a time before taking it up in her small, pale hands.

The serious face Peachie wore did not shift or change. She nodded in silent reverence.

"Keep it clean. It'll take care of ya," Ada said.

The girl spoke low and somber, "I will, Miss Ada. I promise." Peachie turned toward the dark horizon as she rested the rifle's shoulder stock by her leg.

Ada recognized the grim look in the girl's eyes and worried about what the future held.

Worries kept sleep at bay and the night took a quiet and somber turn.

The two filled their days with riding. Ada always made an effort toward pointing out important aspects of the landscape, the pair only stopping occasionally to hunt. Ada demonstrated for Peachie how to find water, what flowers and roots were safe to eat, the importance of staying upwind, and many other survival skills she had learned over the years. The land rolled slowly along under them, the roan unable to do much more than a slow walk with both a grown woman and a young girl upon his back.

Peachie developed a gentle sway in the saddle that matched Ada's, a sway which was born from the gait of the horse.

"Springs only jist rearin' up," Ada observed one day after an hour of quiet riding.

"Touches of death still linger," Peachie added.

Ada cocked an eyebrow. "Yer pretty sharp with words."

"My mama was a school-teacher," Peachie replied. The girl lost herself to thought for a moment before adding, "Mama taught Henri and me all the time."

Ada worried her lip as she remembered her own Louisiana family. "Should be see'n more game soon," Ada said, to break the miserable silence.

"Look!" Peachie perked up. "Deer!" Peachie's finger lingered far to the left of where they rode.

Ada pulled up on the reins and brought the horse to a tree where she looped his reins through the fork in the trunk.

Gloved hand steady as stone, Ada passed Peachie a Colt pistol. Ada then drew the seven-shot Spencer rifle from its leather scabbard. Cautiously, Ada stalked the deer, all the while doing her best to avoid making any sounds or any sudden movements. She stayed on the balls of her feet and moved like an experienced predator. Her muscles were tense, yet she stayed loosed to avoid getting stove up. Fortunately, she was downwind, and the gentle babble of a nearby stream masked her approach.

The deer, a doe, drank nervously from the cold water. The creature was alone, without a buck or fawn for company. The doe's small and fur-covered ears vigilantly twitched and turned.

Ada was closing in at forty yards and just as she was about to make her move—

An old wolf, gnarled, and gray, jumped on Ada. The wolf tore at her limbs while snarling and snapping like a mad creature. The Spencer fired wide as Ada squeezed the trigger on her way to the ground. Startled, the deer turned and fled the commotion deftly and swiftly.

Sharp teeth sank into the thick wool coat Ada had received from Tadita. The wolf's canines pierced the flesh of Ada's arm and a yell of surprise and pain escaped her lips.

Showdown

Ada pressed her back into the ground and fed into the bite, shoving her arm into the maw of the beast, forcing wolf's mouth open to accommodate her. Spittle ran down from the wolf's jaw and along Ada's arm as she grunted and pushed further into the animal in an effort to keep her arm from being shredded.

The wolf growled and heaved as its feet slid underneath it, claws unable to find purchase.

Using her free hand, Ada swung the Spencer like a club and struck the wolf on its head.

The old wolf snarled and snorted. His jaws opened for a quick instant and snapped shut on air when Ada took the advantage and yanked her arm free.

Ada kicked out with her left foot, and her boot struck the wolf in his side.

Twisting his body, the wolf pivoted and latched onto Ada's worn left boot, where his fangs ripped into the hide and punctured Ada's foot.

Ada kicked out with her right foot to try to knock the wolf loose, but ended up only grazing him.

The ground around Ada and the wolf was churned up by their struggle. Dirt covered Ada as she fought and clawed for her life while spitting and cursing with every breath. The wolf shook his muscled neck and tried to tear her foot off.

Eventually, something in Ada's ankle pop. It was a sound she could both feel and hear. Her face paled as she imagined her leg being ripped apart.

Again, Ada cried out as blinding pain shot up her leg. For a split second, she wondered if this would be where she would die. She thought first of herself, then of Peachie as her mind reeled. Water stung Ada's eyes, and she was hoarse from yelling. There was not time to reload the Spencer.

She swung the Spencer with her left hand while holding a stone protruding partway from the soil with her right hand. Her pistol had fallen from her holster at some point during Ada's struggle against the wolf.

The wolf's foamy spittle frothed up as it continued to bite, pull, and snarl fiercely at Ada. His eyes were like death digging into Ada.

As they fought, Ada caught the creeping forms of other wolves closing in. Panic struck her as she could sense her plans for the Preacher and Peachie slipping away.

The roar of gunfire shocked both Ada and the wolf. The echo of a repeat shot blasted near their ears and the wolf fell to its side, its body heavy and heaving. A bloody hole went deep into its side, through a lung, and despite the wolf's repeated attempts to right itself, the animal only shuddered and collapsed. The wolf's breath was ragged and caught as it came out of the animal's large body.

Ada looked up from her bloody boot to see a trembling pair of small and pale hands holding her smoking six-shooter nearby. Peachie dropped the gun and fell to her knees, her small eyes locked on the wolf as Ada took the gun and placed another bullet into the gasping wolf's skull.

Ada peered around as she reached over to Peachie. "Lord, girl. Thank ya," Ada spoke with deep gratitude as she saw the other wolves retreat.

Peachie, her usually fair and rosy face now pale as death itself, could not lift her eyes from the dead wolf before her.

Ada put her arm around Peachie and the girl began to cry silently. As they held one another, a deep feeling of relief washed over them both. As if a dam had burst, Peachie's emotions flooded out.

Time passed, and the Ada and Peachie settled themselves as Peachie's sobs slowly tapered to soft yet exhausted breathing.

Ada pulled back from Peachie. "C'mon girl. Enough tears. I gotta see 'bout this foot."

Peachie helped Ada peel off the shredded boot and pain lanced up Ada's leg. Blood spilled from the boot's collar, and Peachie winced as she tilted the boot and shook the blood from the throat of old leather footwear. Her hands trembled as she tried to steady herself.

Ada caught the girl's eye and said, "Ah'll be alright. Jist need to clean it and bandage it." The wounded woman tried to sound confident but silently hoped they were near a town.

They slowly and with great care cleaned the blood away from Ada's foot and found that the many bite marks were fortunately shallow.

Ada gestured to the water. "Find me some blue or gray clay to pack this."

Peachie looked confused as she walked obediently over to the creek, but returned a few minutes later with a handful of gray river clay.

"Come on," Ada held up her foot, "rub that on me."

The girl took the handfuls of clay and spread it over Ada's foot.

"Ah ain't losin' no parts," Ada said. Ada then ripped herself some strips of bandaging, which Peachie nimbly used to wrap Ada's injuries on her arms, legs, and feet. "Ya done this before?"

Peachie nodded. "My papa showed me. He worked for a doctor in our town."

Ada nodded and allowed the girl to continue tending to her wounds.

"Ada," Peachie spoke hesitantly and with confusion on her face. "Why do you want mud on your foot?"

Ada shrugged. "It's clay. Keeps the gangrene from settin' in."

Peachie nodded.

"Learned 'bout it from the native folk."

At that, a look of surprise crossed Peachie's face.

"Ah'll git moss later," Ada mumbled to herself.

"You saw them? You've talked to them?"

Ada was appreciative, and was comforted by the childish nature of Peachie's questioning. A nature, Ada observed, the young girl kept much repressed.

Ada nodded. "Yea, ah cross paths with 'em here and there." That was all Ada wanted to say of the subject before she tried to stand. The ankle, Ada found, would not bear her weight. She sat on the ground and punched the soil with an angry fist. Ada tore off the other boot and flung it into the nearby brush. "Ain't gonna be another pair like em," Ada mumbled to herself as she rubbed at her temples.

Peachie looked on, but said nothing, not understanding.

Ada caught her look. "Ah can't jist wear one boot, it don't work like that. Ah'd be walkin' in circles and sides. It'd throw off my balance. Ah done many days and nights with bare feet. Sometimes, maybe, ya jist get closer to the land thatta way," Ada tried to explain. Even though she had ridden herd and was a cowgirl, she was a Louisiana swamp girl at heart, some ways days hard.

Taking closer stock of her condition, Ada found that her jacket was torn along the arm and used a knife to cleave the arms from the coat to make it into a vest. The good sleeve she rolled and stored away.

"Maybe ah can make a water skin or sumthin' like that." She cursed and clenched her body, gradually becoming more conscious of how close she'd come to death.

A roar of frustration escaped her and Peachie, startled by the sudden noise, stepped back away from Ada.

The movement caught Ada's eye. "Girl," she sighed, closing her eyes, "ah'm jist frustrated is all. This is gonna slow us down, and we got a ways yet to ride."

Peachie nodded her understanding and chewed her lip.

Again, Ada sighed from her belly with a deep, exasperated breath as she put her eyes on the corpse of the wolf.

"Well," Ada spoke slowly, "may as well clean it." Ada gestured to the wolf. "Pelt ain't much, but meats meat."

Peachie wrinkled her nose and shook her head after remembering the chewy snake they had shared. However, she did not protest further and let Ada walk her through skinning the animal.

"He'll probably be tough and chewy, but it'll do," Ada noted as they laid the skin on the rear of the horse. The meat they took ended up in a bag of salt. Slowly, carefully, and with copious curses, Ada stepped barefoot up into the saddle. She stepped with her good right foot, the side she never stirruped first, before swinging the bandaged leg over the rump of the horse.

Peachie got up easily onto the horse and sat behind Ada, and wrapped her arms loosely around the older woman.

"Almost lost my damn hat again," Ada noted with a grim smile as she adjusted the Stetson.

Peachie sat in a deep silence that stemmed from the events of the day.

"That was some good shootin' back there," Ada commented.

Peachie nodded, but held back from sharing her own thoughts.

As they rode Ada, reconsidered the toughness of the girl she shared her saddle with.

"I prefer the rifle," Peachie mumbled.

Ada nodded in understanding. "Same here. The pistols do in a pinch though."

CHAPTER SEVEN

After the incident with the wolf, the Nebraska Territory was calm and placid. Ada's wounds healed slowly and bothered her less and less. She still had no boots and had to take great care to avoid reopening the tears in her flesh. She leaned on Peachie for meat and for setting up fires. The young girl rose to the challenge as her skills improved and she became more comfortable, and proficient, with survival in the wild.

Peachie often walked next to the horse with her rifle perched on her shoulder. The roan took a liking to Peachie, but she seemed generally more comfortable on her own two feet. Ada could see that the girl's eyes were sharp, and she was doing well at keeping a lookout both for game and for any sign of Henri. At night, Ada would listen to the girl praying in French for the safety of her brother as she drifted off to a fitful rest. After listening to her, Ada even started offering up small prayers for her family and, occasionally, for William.

As they approached the Colorado Territory, Ada could feel the tension mounting deep in her bones. "Gettin closer. Leadin' us to the ranch," Ada spoke to herself, low and steady.

Peachie shot Ada a quizzical look and then asked in a halting tone, "Why did this man kill my parents?" "Why did her take Henri?"

They rode slow and steady in an even four-beat gait. As they continued on, Ada thought about how to explain the cursed

Preacher to Peachie. She wondered how could she explain such evil to this girl. Ada, usually at no loss for words, clenched her jaw and squeezed the pommel.

"He killed my folks too," Ada eventually told Peachie. "Much the same way as yours."

The blood seemed to drain from Peachie's face and down her neck as her eyes went wide and disbelieving, while her small head softly shook from side to side.

Ada's mind drifted to her dark childhood memories. Images of her Ma and Pa laying in their own blood with their throats slit filled her mind and made her head spin.

"But why Henri?" Peachie eventually softly inquired.

Ada shook her head in frustrated consternation. It was all too familiar. "Ah can't say. That man's evil walking upon the earth," Ada answered truthfully.

Peachie stared ahead past Ada as she tried to keep her eyes dry.

Ada placed a consoling hand on the girl's knee. "We'll git 'im," Ada spat as she sat chewing her lip.

Nodding, the girl's worried eyes scanned the horizon in desperation.

Not long after, the roan came upon a thick barrier of brush near a small creek and shied at the thick, hard foliage.

"Gotta go through there, boy," Ada urged him on in the hope his trust in her would be enough to see them to the end. The Cajun woman stood in the saddle and sized up the landscape from the back of the horse. "It stretches fer a bit," she observed. Ada saw no way around and shook her head as she readied herself for the passage.

At Ada's insistence, the horse made its way through the brambles. Ada held the reins tight and steered him through the safest path.

A small object on the ground caught Peachie's sharp eye, and she rose up a cheer, "That's Henri's shoe!"

Ada's firm arm held the girl back before she jumped down from the saddle. "Leave it, these here briars will cut ya up sumthin' bad." Ada's steely and sharp eyes scanned the brush but found no other sign of Peachie's brother. It was at this time that she realized unbandaged foot was being lacerated by the thorns and when she looked down she also saw shallow cuts on the roan's chest and legs. The horse's blood was a deep red and ran in thin lines down to his hooves.

A pang of guilt ran through Ada at the understanding that her horse was wounded and she made a silent promise that he would give him some rest soon. They continued their way through the dangerous terrain; it was a slow process through thick and unwelcoming plant life. It was a narrow divide that took them more time than Ada planned for.

"They sure came this way, but didn't linger none," Ada observed.

Peachie pursed her lips and squinted as if willing her brother into view.

The thickening brush funneled them through a small slice in the land before the brambles finally gave way to rocks and those rocks gave way to stone walls. The shallow canyon walls were low and banal. A smooth, empty, and sheer blue sky lingered a few feet above Ada's head. The walls came in close to the roan and just as they reached his flanks, they parted again.

It was at this time that a claustrophobic crack opened up into a wide, flat area filled with dirt, large stones, and the occasional hardy ironwood shrub. As Ada and Peachie emerged back into the open, returning to a place where they had a wide-open blue sky above them, they heard voices along with the clanging and banging sounds bouncing off the walls behind them.

"That bastard did nothin' to help," a gruff voice declared as the noisy din continued.

Ada was confused since it sounded like a blacksmith's hammer ringing out.

"The coins are real," said the gruff voice with a cough.

"Ain't no worry of his, what comes of us," a nasally voice followed.

Ada led the horse through the large boulders while seeking the source of the conversation and racket.

The red-speckled horse rounded a large boulder and Ada suddenly found herself coming upon the two men she'd heard. She glanced over at them and spotted the busted chain that had obviously once held them together.

Startled, the men threw their stones at the horse and its two riders. The flying rocks caused the horse to spin and step away from the two men, but luckily, none of the hastily thrown projectiles struck Ada, Peachie, or the horse.

"What the hell?" Ada hollered at the pair as she worked to steady her horse.

Ada drew her pistol, and Peachie had the rifle out on the saddle boot as soon as the horse had steadied.

The young girl wrinkled her nose at the men whose clothes and hair were caked with filth.

The four eyed one another. The two men gripped more stones, but launched none.

"Put that shit down," Ada commanded while gesturing to the men with her Colt.

A wide-eyed glance was exchanged by the men after they looked Ada over.

"That's her," said the gruff-voiced man as he gestured to Ada with a nod of his head.

Both men grabbed another stone and poised themselves to spring.

"What in the Sam Hill is wrong with y'all? Ah'll shoot y'all down right now if'n you do anythin' funny!" Ada spoke with a severity that left no doubt as to what she would do.

Casting eyes to each other and then the ground, the men dropped their arms in defeat, the short chains on iron cuffs dangling from their sleeves glinting in the sunlight.

Each of the men deposited the stones they held with a flat thud.

"We ain't gonna do you nuthin' at all," the smaller man with the nasally voice spoke up.

"Ya sure looked like ya was doin sumthin when ya was throwin' rocks at us," Ada pointed out while pointing her Colt for emphasis. "Who are y'all and what the hell are ya doin' out here?"

The man with the nasally voice spoke up first and said, "I'm Ezekiel. This here is Jebediah."

The other man nodded tightly without taking his dark eyes off Ada.

The man named Ezekiel wrung his hands and wore a worried look up on face.

Ada cocked her pistol, and Peachie held her Spencer steady. "Alight, so that's who y'all are, but what are y'all on about?" Ada said, with a steel edge to her voice and stark eyes that held the men in place.

"Ain't nuthin' ma'am," Ezekiel said. "We was in a convoy that got waylaid by them native folk. Everyone else got themselves kilt. We came thisaway past them briars and come out here. That other fella yonder. . ." Ezekiel shifted his weight as his voice trailed off.

The convicts avoided Ada's eyes by looking at the ground, then the sky, then the boulder.

Ada sighed in frustration. "Well, out with it, dammit!" She encouraged the man to speak with a gesture of her weapon.

Ezekiel and Jebediah exchanged a glance before Ezekiel sputtered out, "He paid us to waylay ya here!"

Ada hunkered down into the saddle and turned her gaze south. Her mild reaction made both men visibly relax.

"We jist want to git outta this here is all," Ezekiel stated. He shook his arm, and the chain rattled sharply.

The other man, Jebediah, added, "You can take the money. Ain't got no need for it. Would ya help us cut these off, though?" He held up the iron cuff bound to his wrist.

To Ada's eyes, Jebediah looked offended and embarrassed by the chain and the situation. Something about him reminded her of her grandfather. There was something old and dignified in the dark, gruff man.

Ada sighed and shook her head, her long hair moving languidly across Peachie's face. "Girl, ya reckon can hit them cuffs?"

"I'm not too sure about that, but I will try," Peachie said, as she measured the shot in perfect stillness.

The men's eyes widened into saucers as they realized what Ada was suggesting.

A small wicked smile crept over Ada's face as the two men floundered and began to stammer nonsense, sweat visibly beginning to form on both of the men's brows.

"Hold girl. Ah could use the bounties y'all would bring. If'n these fellas get kilt, ah can't collect no reward," Ada proclaimed, loud enough for everyone to hear.

"Ain't no reward on us, mam. We was heading to hang without trial. The warden probably think us dead along with the rest. They'll find them dead men soon enough. Ain't no bounty on us, only sin," said Jebediah.

A warm wind blew from the south as Ada and Peachie sized up the two strangers. It sent a comfortable feeling of home over the Cajun woman. Ada's heart gave a brief leap to her chest as she felt the familiar pull calling her back to her ranch. It revitalized her and made her eager to ride past all this. The wind tousled the roan mane and ran through Ada's clothes as it dissipated and left them behind to continue on its journey to somewhere far beyond the horizon.

Ada stepped down out of the saddle and walked over to the two strange men. "Set ya arm here on this here rock and ah'll blast them irons off," Ada instructed.

Ezekiel and Jebediah shared a glance.

"Alight, Miss—" Jebediah started as he walked over the Ada.

"Ada Picou," she said as she tapped the barrel of the Colt against the hinge on the cuff. The man did not flinch when Ada fired the single shot that broke the man free of his irons.

Jebediah rubbed at his wrist as he gestured to the waiting Ezekiel.

"Don't shoot me mam," Ezekiel pleaded with a voice as shaky as his hands.

Ada narrowed her eyes and popped off another round.

Ezekiel jerked his hand at the sound and the cuff fell to the dirt below him.

Quickly Ada thumbed two rounds into the cylinder, fully believing the men would lunge for her now that they were free.

However, they did not.

Peachie held her rifle at the ready and had a bead on both men.

"Now, you gents don't try nuthin' funny," Ada stated, considering the fact that she had just set free two criminals.

"Thank you, mam," Ezekiel said as he rubbed at his neck and shook his legs while doing a slight turn in an odd dance.

Jebediah tilted his head to Ada. "Thank you, mam, we are

much obliged."

Ada considered tipping her Stetson to the man, but instead narrowed her eyes and gave him a tight nod. "Which way was he headed?" Ada pressed the men as she stepped back up and into the saddle.

Ezekiel frowned, and after a moment, pointed southwest.

"Was my brother with him?" Peachie blurted out.

Jebediah lifted both eyebrows before he solemnly, and with a sad expression, spoke. "He was miss. Boy looked fair. A might tuckered out and hungry, I'd say is all," he said.

Peachie's eyes went wide and focused on the horizon ahead.

Ada felt that she'd become closer to Peachie of late, but could not allow herself to forget the goal that held them together would soon be accomplished. She couldn't allow their friendliness to lead to any deeper attachments.

Jebediah held out his hand toward Ada, and in it, Ada noticed coins.

"What fer?" Ada asked.

"We was paid with this. We ain't for murder'n nobody. Just takin' what we need to survive," Jebediah stated flatly.

Ada shook her head disapprovingly. "Jist steer clear'a that man." She eyed the men with a cold and grim look. "And us," she added.

"We surely will mam, turned my blood cold, he did." Jebediah said. The man shivered even though the air was warm.

Ada looked the two men over and then turned the roan just in time to notice a glimmer of light at the distant horizon. "Down!" Ada yelled.

Ada threw Peachie off the horse and onto the hard earth. She shifted her body to the side of the horse and pulled him to the ground too, bringing him into crouch upon the ground before forcing him onto his side by pressing her hands upon his neck to still him in all the commotion. After all their years together, the horse trusted Ada. Although his eyes stayed wide, he did not fight her.

Meanwhile, Ezekiel hit the ground flat on his belly and raised up a small dust cloud.

Peachie's face was stark white as she searched the horizon wildly.

Blood spurted from Jebediah and he let out a cry as the red dotted the nearby ground in a glistening crimson.

The rapport of a rifle echoed off the walls just behind the small group.

Ezekiel muttered prayers, his tears barely held back as he tried to crawl to Jebediah, but lost his strength to terror.

Ada squinted in the direction she had spotted the glint of sunlight on metal, but saw nothing more in the distance.

Ezekiel slightly rose as he lurched over to Jebediah.

"Stay the hell down!" Ada yelled.

Dirt shot into the air near the moving man. The puff of dirt appeared innocently and covered its malice. The flat clap of the distant gun followed.

"Now be still, ya damn coot!" Ada swore and cursed under her breath as, heart racing, beads of sweat stung at her eyes. She knew their group was pinned down and trapped, as well as that Jebediah was bleeding out despite the hands pressed to his gut as he tried to stymie his lifeblood before any more of it flowed out onto the rocks and dirt.

"Fire and damnation, he's got us cornered her y'all. Stay the hell down and don't move none. Peachie, ya alright girl?" Ada clenched her jaw into a grimace as she tried to come up with some way to keep Peachie and her horse safe. Having seen gut wounds like Jebediah's before, Ada hoped the dying man would not linger, but would give up the ghost peacefully.

"I am," Peachie said from a few feet away.

"Don't ya move now," Ada instructed.

Peachie nodded to the cowpoke and did her best not to look at Jebediah as the pool of red about the man swiftly grew.

"Jeb!" Ezekiel cried out as he reached the other man.

"Zeke, find sumthin and do some good. Do it for both of us,"

Jebediah voice cracked and faded as his spirit left him.

Ada heard no more shots being fired, but was wary to move just yet. She dropped her head to the ground when Jebediah passed. She knew she could have done nothing, but felt guilt nonetheless. "Damn that blued eyed beast to hell," she cursed.

Peachie's hand found Ada's, and the two slowly moved together behind the horse.

They lay that way until the sun finished its descent toward the horizon.

At dusk, Ada stood slowly and raised the stiff roan. "Good job, boy," Ada said as she patted him down and the roan shook his head, his flanks quivering at Ada's touch. Turning her attention to Peachie, Ada said, "Girl, ya gonna be alright." it was a statement, not a question.

Peachie nodded, yet trembled as her eyes locked on the two men hunched over in the dark sand.

Ada patted her horse. "Ah won't do that again if ah can help it." She talked to the horse as she walked him over to Peachie. "Hold him," she said, handing the girl the reins before making her way over to the two convicts.

Ezekiel was laying splayed out next to Jebediah's white corpse. The older and gruffer man was dead, the thirsty ground around him dark with his blood. Ezekiel was shaking and whispering something to himself and when he noticed Ada nearing, the convict pressed the eyes of the man named Jebediah forever closed.

Ezekiel turned a pleading eye to Ada and stated, "I got to bury him. If'n you all could help, maybe?"

Ada looked once more into the dark. She knew she would see no sign of the Preacher until he wanted her to, and that chasing him tonight would only needlessly tire her. With a sigh, she nodded to Ezekiel.

Ada and Ezekiel dragged Jebediah's body to a small and dark niche in the stone wall of the canyon whence Ada and Peachie had emerged.

Peachie stood watch with a cold sweat on her brow and held the Spencer at the ready as the two adults pulled down rocks to form a makeshift grave.

Ada turned to the girl and said, "He's leadin' us back to my ranch."

Peachie furrowed her brow, and the look made Ada feel a great burden of guilt.

"Ah'm sorry Zeke," Ada softly offered the strange convict.

Ezekiel nodded and patted Ada on the arm as he walking away from her and the makeshift grave site, heading into the darkness of the wilds to be alone with his thoughts.

CHAPTER EIGHT

Ada vividly remembered the prior season and the cold bitterness of the winter when she had been left for dead, shot by the Preacher in the Dakota Territory. At the time, she had inflicted him with injury as well.

"Must a known ah'd make it," Ada said as she rubbed her thigh with her fist until her knuckles were white. "Could be he heard ah was laid up at the fort." The powerful force of speculation grew in Ada's mind.

She thumbed the small dog carving Beautiful Doe, a medicine woman in the Dakota Territory, had carved it for Ada. To Ada, it served as a reminder of the ranch, William, and that stray blue heeler, who had strayed to their ranch and taken them both in to his trust. She had not recognized the importance of the thing until the Preacher had put his attention on the figure.

As though struck by lightning, Ada realized she had been hunted across the snowy wastes as much as she had done the hunting. The carving made her keenly aware of the Preacher's intent. Whether he had intended for her to find the tossed-aside figure or not, she knew where his mind was bent. Both Ada and the Preacher were burning coal and racing to the ranch, where they were fated for a collision.

"William's in danger 'cause of me," Ada muttered to herself while thinking back to the fight in Mr. Guilford Grimshaw's office near her ranch in New Mexico.

After hunting the Preacher for years, only to walk into the office and beat the man soundly, she knew their paths were intertwined. The Preacher was repeating his old ways just like when he had been hired to kill her parents and brother because of land. The two enemies had spent more than an entire season hunting each other in the snowy hellscape of the Dakota Territory in the dead cold of winter. The Preacher was intent on creating suffering for her, it seemed to Ada, like his will was set upon it.

"Why are we cursed with this demon?" Ada asked herself under her breath. She turned and caught Peachie's curious eye upon her.

Both kidnapping the boy and leaving the girl was a cruel reminder of Ada's own life's tragedy. Sitting up on the red roan with Peachie, Ada bit her lip and turned her eye away from the girl. She planned to avoid a direct route.

"Any luck, we won't get bushwhacked if we stay a bit wide of his trail," she mumbled.

Peachie looked at Ada with concern and worry on her face.

Ada unclenched her jaw just enough to grumble, "We'll git him, dammit."

The red roan headed southwest at a slow and steady walk. Ada caught Peachie looking behind them occasionally at Ezekiel, who was following them. There was an air of neglect upon the man thanks to the thick layer of soil on his overalls and the floppy hat that may have been part of an animal at some point.

The girl looked up at Ada and said, "I think Mr. Ezekiel is following us."

Ada shrugged and sighed. "Yea, seems so."

The trio trudged along at a slow pace, set by a combination of weariness and watchfulness. Distance grew between the man and the two who rode on the horse. After a spell, they heard Ezekiel yell behind them.

"Hold on, wait fir me!" Ezekiel shouted.

Ada pulled at the reins and stopped the large red roan.

The man huffed over to the horse as Ada and Peachie waited, their patience tested.

Ada frowned down at Ezekiel. "There ain't much room here on this here horse fer nobody else."

"I'll walk, I'm spry." Ezekiel smiled with a snaggle-toothed grin and shrugged.

Ada noted his bloodshot eyes and the dark circles hanging under them.

"Five years we was together," Ezekiel prattled on as he walked. "Five long and hot years w broke stone, drove rails, cut wood. . . you name it," Ezekiel spoke low. He looked off to the sky and threw out his arms before shouting to Heaven,

"We done did it all!"

Peachie watched the strange old man with curious interest while Ada kept her eyes ahead, not wanting to encourage his behavior. Still, she found herself setting a slower pace for the man's convenience even as her eyes constantly searched the horizon for another deadly glint of iron.

Ada stole a glance down at Ezekiel as they moved slowly across the warming landscape. "Ah ain't givin' ya no gun," she said with finality.

Ezekiel nodded and shook his head while holding his hands open and upward. He seemed to agree easily enough, and Ada frowned at him in mild confusion.

"Where we headed?" Ezekiel asked.

"Colorado," Ada answered tersely. "Then down to the New Mexico territory," she added flatly.

The man nodded and chewed at a branch he had pulled off a pecan tree.

"Everyone giving us a wide berth," Ada noted of the few other travelers they passed. She looked at herself, her two companions, and the horse over. "Must be a damn sight," she muttered.

Cool, crisp night made way for a gentle warm breeze that drifted in from the south. The wind carried with it the faint smell of dust and the wilds of Mexico.

The horse was rubbed down, there was a small fire smoldering down to embers, and the three unlikely travelers sat together in tense silence.

Ezekiel turned to Peachie and struck up a conversation by starting with, "Where you from?" "You talk funny," he added with a scrunched-up face.

There was a moment where only the wind carried a sound, and Peachie eyed the man through slitted eyes. Peachie soon turned to look at Ada, and the experienced and worldly bounty hunter nodded, her hair dancing in the breeze without her hat to cover it.

"France," Peachie said, turning up her nose at him and sitting ramrod straight.

Ezekiel laughed with a big smile and bright eyes, which only made the girl's neck and face redder.

"Where are *you* from?" Peachie asked with clear disdain. "You speak like an inbred," she added harshly. As the words left her mouth, she felt the guilt of having ignored his loss and suffering.

EzekielHe flinched, squinted at herPeachie, and scratched his nose. "I don't rightly know what that is, but I'm from South Carolina, not wherever this 'Inbred place is," he answered simply.

Ada shook her head in exasperation at the two odd folks she

rode with.

Ezekiel pulled a handful of dandelions and wild asparagus from a pocket in his trousers. "That ain't no real place, France," he sniggered to himself as he took a bite of the foraged foodstuff.

Ada and Peachie shared a glance of confusion.

"It's a real place Zeke," Ada stated as she worked a piece of wood with one of her knives.

"Yeah, right past Big Rock Candy Mountain," Ezekiel stated before chuckling to himself.

Again, both Ada and Peachie exchanged a confused look. Ezekiel paused his laughter and looked into their eyes, matching their confusion.

In the stillness that followed, the only disturbance was that made by the wind and the horse.

Ada tilted her head back and her gaze drifted up to the stars.

"*I know a place,*" Ezekiel began singing in a messy way while chewing through the roadside spoils.

"What the hell," Ada started. An angry look passed over her face as Ezekiel continued singing, ignoring everything else but his mirth.

A smile grew on Peachie's face and her teeth flashed a moment before she hid her quiet laughter behind her hand.

Ada rolled her eyes as she settled back down and held up her flask.

Ezekiel beamed and sang louder for a time before his singing faltered and he nodded off.

The three wanderers suddenly finding themselves thrown together into a ragtag group found sleep without nightmares that night.

The morning found the three fresh and braced for another day of travel. Ezekiel continued to talk up a storm, making a noteworthy contrast to Ada's quiet ways of moving over the countryside. Peachie enjoyed the conversation and showed signs of starting to warm up to the convict's strange ways.

"Texas is flat like a flapjack," Ezekiel said as he walked.

"We ain't in Texas," Ada stated in agitation.

Ezekiel shrugged. "Still as flat. There ain't no mountains here, and there ain't and no big gorges neither. What is there, but emptiness and flat ground as far as the eye can see?"

Occasionally, Ada and Peachie walked alongside the roan to give him a respite from their weight, an easy feat while they hobbled along at Ezekiel's meandering pace.

Ada watched the way Peachie and Ezekiel moved as they traveled together, what they looked at, and listened to their

rambling and sometimes nonsensical talks. Ada knew that she could learn about her traveling companions from what they did, and did not, say.
Wisps of light brown hair framed Peachie's wind-blown face, while most of the rest of it was tied up in a strange knot at the back of her head. Ada thought that the hat Peachie wore must have come from the girl's father, considering that it was too big and the girl never took it off. The battered, sun-bleached brown hat had seen better days, but Peachie clung to it.

They shared a similar history; a fact Ada took special note of as she patted the flask in her pocket. She remembered her father drinking from it on special occasions and found a small comfort in the memory. A holdover from the war, her mother said, although she knew there was more to it.

The woman from Louisiana looked down at the girl from France as she walked near the horse. Peachie wore coarse and yet well-made broadcloth trousers and a shirt. Her coat appeared home spun and her shoes were decent leather. Ada noted the care put into the stitching and realized that the child's parents must have been craftspeople of some type.

"Yer ma sewed?" Ada gestured to Peachie's clothes.

The girl thought for a moment and nodded. "She taught, and she sewed what we had. My father helped. He said he knew stitching from sewing people up."

"Yeah, ma Pa learnt in the war. He'd sit with my Ma and mend our clothes," Ada said.

"You helped?" Peachie asked.

Ada nodded silently and thought back to the times she and brother sat with their parents at night in the glow of the fire doing small tasks together.

"I sewed my own clothes, too. Just I ain't no good at it," stated Ezekiel, reminding Ada and Peachie he was there. Ezekiel trudged along in dirty clothes that had not known color in ages. To Ada's eye, the man presented the exact opposite visage of the young girl.

"Zeke, ya'd be filthy in a hurricane," Ada finally pointed out.

He smiled knowingly. "Keeps my smell from the animals."

Ada had let Ezekiel hunt with her occasionally as they traveled. Not only was he an exceptional hunter, but he dressed his kills well.

Peachie watched as Ezekiel hefted stones into the air. "Where did you learn to hunt like that, Zeke?" Peachie asked, in reference to how he had pelted down two ducks with just stones.

"My brother. We used to hunt all the time, we fished too. My folks didn't like me lingering around the house too much 'cause I broke stuff a lot. My brother looked out for me," Ezekiel answered.

"Well, he did a good job. You are a good shot," Peachie complimented the man.

Ezekiel looked at Ada with a sheepish grin.

"Ya still ain't gettin' no gun," Ada said.

He shrugged and said, "Never bothered me none. My pappy never let me shoot none. Couldn't never get'em to go straight."

Luck struck when eventually Ada spotted wild sheep on their route. She signaled to Peachie to draw the rifle from the boot and the girl spring into action.

Swinging down from the saddle, Peachie braced herself on a rocky outcropping and drew a bead on a ram just under a hundred yards away. Ada watched with a calculating eye the girl's every move as she breathed out of the shot.

The next moment, the ram dropped and the others scattered.

The young girl from France looked up at Ada and Ada nodded to her in approval.

The roan took Ada to the kill, and she brought that animal back to Peachie on his croup.

"Ya done good, girl," Ada said as she pulled the ram from the horse.

Peachie scrunched up her face and shook her head. "I can't clean it!" She visibly paled at the implication in Ada's actions.

Ada sighed and pulled out her skinning knife. She knew that Peachie, a hard worker and a good shot, still had no stomach for dressing a kill. "Zeke, git over here and give me a hand,"

Ada directed as Peachie became sick in a nearby swale.

Peachie watched them work from afar as the two elder members of their group cleaned the big-horned sheep.

"Ya do alright Zeke." Ada left him to finishing carving up the meat as she dragged her knife over the creature's hide.

"I was the one who found food for me and Jeb. He was learnt and didn't know nuthin' about foragin' or huntin' in the world," Ezekiel said sadly.

"Ya gotta watch it with these bigger ones." Ada gestured to the sheep after getting Peachie's attention.

"Gotta eat some greens with it," Ezekiel chimed in.

"He's right," Ada agreed.

"Why?" Peachie inquired.

"Meat poisoning," Ada said simply as she splayed the hide flat in the sun.

"Makes ya crazy," Ezekiel said as he started singing something low, silly, and off-key. He winked at the young girl and she shook her head. He often sang odd shanties and jigs, almost always at the most inopportune moments.

Ada watched the exchange while cooking some of the bits of ram at the edge of her knife and thought about how often she had seen the man talking to himself. She also heard him having one-sided conversations, seemingly with Jebediah. She looked over the fire as she slowly turned the sizzling meat on her blade.

"Zeke, tell me about Jebediah," Peachie said out of the blue.

Ezekiel looked at her, frowned, and then dropped his eyes to the ground. Shaking his head, he said, "No, I can't rightfully do that now," and shuffled over to a dark corner of the campsite.

Ada put her hand on Peachie's shoulder. "Don't press him none."

Peachie looked down at her feet with pain on her face.

Ada gave Peachie a small pat on the shoulder, and Peachie nodded and raised her eyes to the stars.

"Like my mother and father," Peachie whispered in understanding.

"Yeah, like that." Ada felt guilt of her own toward the child before her.

That night Ezekiel slept alone beyond the flickering light of the fire's illuminating reach.

As the night darkened, Peachie turned to Ada who was staring to the south.

"Ya ruminating about yer brother, ain't ya?" Ada asked.

"I am. It hurts, I miss him so much." Peachie said as she took Ada's hand and they sat in silence while waiting for sleep.

"Ah miss mine too," Ada said in low close to the girl's ear. "We gonna git yer brother back. Ahmma end that man," Ada said in a voice that was grim and determined.

Ada knew the devil they trailed and the concerns she had were rooted in her years of experience hunting him. She knew he would kill all three of them, and everyone she was connected to, with hardly a thought. She could not understand why he was intent upon her and her personal suffering. Ada knew the Preacher was aware of her hunting him after the Dakotas, but the way he acted wasn't just to shake her, it was to make her suffer.

Ada wondered what was in that dark heart of his. "He ain't jist lookin' for revenge for cleanin' his clock in New Mexico."

"How do you know?" Peachie asked, quietly bringing Ada out of the wandering solitude of her mind.

Ada looked at the girl and answered, "Cus ah'm persistent."

The group said little to each other as they packed up just before dawn the next morning. Just as they were finishing up, the echo of a single gunshot reached their camp. Another quickly followed.

Ada cringed and flexed her fists and toes. Her eyes met Peachie's, and the fear in the girl's expression drove Ada to double-check her loaded rounds.

Minutes later, the red roan was carrying Ada and Peachie, with Ezekiel walking alongside, through the rolling landscape. Ada kept her silver sharp eyes peeled for danger.

Everyone was on edge and waiting for whatever might strike next.

CHAPTER NINE

The fierce woman from Louisiana detected no telltale dust clouds, or glints of steel in the distance. Flat and dry air surrounding them was devoid of the smell of smoke and the sounds of gunfire they had heard earlier was not repeated as Ada, Peachie, and Ezekiel slowly made their way south and west, toward the sound of the original gunshot. Three pairs of eyes darted in all directions in search of threats among the small cholla and gangly mesquite. The land had a gentle roll to it and obscured their view of the horizon on occasion until, after reaching the top of a rise, the trio spotted a small building in the distance.

"What's that?" Peachie said first. She pointed ahead of them, her finger drawing the attention of her companions to the west.

"Not sure." Ada squinted at the structure as she pulled up the horse.

"We'll find out in a bit," Ezekiel said while attempting to keep the anxiousness out of his voice despite how He shifted his weight from foot to foot nervously as he walked.

"Well, ah reckon we should take a look." Ada clicked to the roan and started him off, walking toward the building in the distance.

Peachie and Ezekiel nodded hesitantly, their eyes not leaving the small and ramshackle building.

The building was further away than the small group first judged thanks to the way the open land played tricks on their senses.

"It's quiet out here," Ezekiel muttered under his breath as they trudged along in the warm sunlight.

Ada spotted a rattlesnake to their left, but kept moving without giving the sunbathing creature a second thought after it uncoiled its body and sidled into a nearby hole.

Peachie squeezed the pommel with her left-hand and one arm around Ada's waist, Peachie's rifle balanced at her hip and gripped tightly in her right hand. Ada had drawn a six-shooter and held the reins loose, her eyes watching the roan's ears as much as she scanned the terrain ahead of them. Even the roan was tense in his gait.

As they approached the small building, they could see the age worn into its features. Boards were cracked, dry, and bleached gray by the sun. There were chips missing from the edges of planks and large gaps between the boards. There were no windows, just a small door that led into darkness. As they rode closer, the barrel of a gun poked from the opening.

"Git, ya'll!" A man's voice yelled to them, "Want no trouble here. Move along!"

"We ain't here fir trouble, mister," Ada shouted calmly, yet the group still froze in the face of the stranger's threatening air.

"A woman, eh?" Came the voice from beyond the door.

Peachie spoke up surprising Ada, "Yes, sir. We are just passing through and we do not want any trouble. *S'il vous plaît?*" Peachie pleaded.

"Ya'll a motley sight, ain't ya?" The man's voice was gravelly, and held a drawl. "You Yanks? You all Frenchies like this one?"

"Nah, my Pa fought for Jefferson," answered Ada.

the man emerged slowly from the shadows and had his rifle lowered. "I'll be damned," the man said as he came into the light.

"Darn, you old," Ezekiel blurted out earning a cutting look from Ada and Peachie.

The old man spat into the dirt and gave Ezekiel a wicked look of his own while lifting the barrel of his rifle a hair. The man stood at about five feet and was covered in sun-bleached grays. Even his wispy hair was gray, a stark contrast to the dark and leathery look of his wrinkled face.

"Damn sight, y'all three there," the man said as he scratched his ear.

Ezekiel had his hat in his hands and wrung it nervously, while Peachie sat quietly and with her back straight in front of Ada. Ada tapped the Spencer and Peachie slid it back into the scabbard.

"Sorry ta bother ya, but we're tailin' a fella. Heard shots this'a way." Ada gestured casually to the building.

The grizzled old man pea-cocked, "No need ta worry over me, that other fella though—"

"Was he in black and was there a young boy with him?" Peachie interrupted.

The old man looked at Peachie, and after a pause, nodded and narrowed his eyes.

Ada caught the wild-eyed worry on Peachie's face. "He was all in black, like a preacher?" Ada asked to confirm.

The man rubbed at his jaw before he spoke and the wind rustled his old gray coat. "He weren't no preacher. I'm damn sure a that," said the old man. He then sat heavily upon a dry crate that was on the stoop. "Tried to kill me hisself." The man's thick fingers deftly pulled a tin from one of his pockets and he set some tobacco on his lip. His gaze took in Ada, Peachie, and Ezekiel, the curiosity obvious in his stare. "Where's yer boots?" The man gestured to Ada's dirty feet.

"Worn out," Ada answered plainly.

The man nodded and then said forlornly, "Happened in the war too often." His thick shoulders sagged as he sighed.

"Come on down," he gestured for Peachie and Ada to step down from the horse and, when they did, he continued, "Put him over there." The old man pointed to a small fenced-in paddock at the rear of the building.

Ada walked the roan over and led him through the gate. She removed the halter, bridle, and saddle.

Peachie carried the tack to the fence and placed it on the top post. In the paddock was a small patch of green and a shaggy old mule. The man nodded in satisfaction at the care Peachie and Ada showed the roan and the tack.

"Now ya'll behave," Ada patted both animals before closing the gate behind her. Leaving the horse, the duo rejoined Ezekiel and the old man on the porch.

"May I feed them?" Peachie asked the old man.

He looked at her and nodded. "Go on ahead, little miss Frenchie." He gestured to the sack of corn near the porch.

When Peachie returned to the paddock, she found the roan and mule did not appear to mind the company and both appeared happy to smell the corn.

"Whatcha do," the old man asked Ezekiel while giving him a side-eyed glance.

Ezekiel squinted at the sun and shifted his weight around as he sat on the loose wooden planks.

Ezekiel reminded Ada of a moth in a jar.

Ezekiel looked at Ada and Peachie when the duo returned. Neither spoke, preferring to watch casually. Ada gave the convict a small nod and, with that reassurance, Ezekiel spoke slowly with many pauses that made Ada think he was trying to remember and forget his past at the same time.

". . .I didn't know he was a hunter. He was a government man," he said. Ezekiel looked down at his hands. "I didn't kill him, though. I was there with my brother and. . . he took me."

The grizzled old man turned a questioning eye to Ada.

Ada gave a slight shrug of her shoulder.

"Jeb said I'd be forgiven," Ezekiel said as he shifted his weight and leaned his head to the side. "We was in all white and dussed up like."

Ada gradually realized what had happened, the things she'd yet to learn, and she sucked her teeth.

"My brother, he said, 'Zeke, we gotta fix a man up' just like that." Ezekiel paused and shook his head. "I didn't know him none. Was Republican."

The old man spat, drawing a dirty look from Peachie. "Damn Yanks," the old man stated.

Ada looked back at Ezekiel and gave him a slight tilt of her head for him to continue.

"He was shot." Ezekiel looked at the ground and choked a bit on his words before they came out. "He danced first," he added softly. "It was bad. He got robbed too." Ezekiel's eyes were bloodshot and appeared to worsen the longer he looked to the ground. "I didn't know anyone was gonna die," his voice lowered, and he balled his hands into fists. "When it happened, I ran. I threw that old white sheet and ran with all I had." He sighed deeply and his barrel chest shook slightly.

Peachie looked back at the paddock with her brow beetled.

"I ran from South Carolina as quick as I could and I kept on running from there." Ezekiel wiped at his face with his dirty sleeve. "I jist ran with no sense of where I was headed. That's when I met up with Jeb," Ezekiel stated. Head low and voice lower, he groaned, "We was on the lamb together." Ezekiel coughed on some dust and stopped talking.

"Is that why you were arrested?" Peachie eventually broke the silence.

Ezekiel shook his head without meeting the young girl's eyes. "Jebediah was wanted for makin' money with a pressin' or sumthin." Ezekiel shrugged to indicate his lack of understanding. "We got caught in Nebraska by a deputy. Thought we was cavort'n."

Ada rocked back on her calloused heels and pursed her lips. She stole a glance at Peachie's face and noted how the girl was openly confused.

"Hold on now," the old man spoke up and leaned in, his eyes screwing up as he took in Ezekiel's meek posture. He had propped his gun against the doorjamb at some point while Ezekiel was telling his story. "You saying you wasn't arrested for murder, but fornicat'n?"

Ada shook her head slightly at the strange story.

"We was caught foraging for food in a barn, so that's the sum of it," Ezekiel answered. "I didn't mean fer nobody to git kill't."

"Boy, did ya have a gun that night," the old man asked as he leaned back against the wall.

Ezekiel tightened his eyes and answered, "No sir," shaking his head.

Silence followed. The quiet was broken by the grating and coarse laughter of the old man.

"I'll be damned," he chuckled roughly. "Ya'll are welcome to stay the night," he said before standing and turning to go inside. "A story like that'll get you a meal, meager as it is." He nodded to Ezekiel and extended his hand to pull the other man up from the dry and cracked porch planks. "Name is Lewis. Lewis Barrios," the old man said as he turned his sun-seared cheeks to look at Ada. "What are you called?"

"Ada Picou, this here is Adelle—"

"Adelle Duran," Peachie nodded formally.

Lewis tipped his hat.

Ada sighed. "Ya already been acquainted with Ezekiel."

Ezekiel, after patting the dust from his dirty and ragged clothes, introduced himself. "Ezekiel Dail," he said proudly.

Showdown

The three followed Lewis inside, exhausted and hungry.

CHAPTER TEN

Wind cut through the small drafty building that looked to be held together with dust. Bleached, pale, weathered, and brittle wooden walls were strung together with rusted old square nails. There was no window to let in the light. Still, there was enough to see by as long as the door was ajar. A lantern glowed from atop a crate that supposedly stored supplies and sat ready for the coming dark of evening. A spindly lizard scurried out the door as the humans entered.

"Welcome, strangers, to my humble abode," Lewis said with a laugh that was dry and clipped.

Ada stepped into the room and said, "nice place ya got. Thanks, friend. We appreciate the shade." Ada said, as Peachie and Ezekiel sat down on the dusty boards.

Ada's hip burned as she lowered herself to the floor herself and the group braced their backs against the thin boards of the walls. In the corner was piled some bedding where Lewis set himself heavily down, his body and the surrounding wood creaking and cracking as he did so.

A fine layer of dust lifted as they sat, the countless motes sparkling in the thin shafts of light.

The old man squared his shoulders and looked Ada in the eye. "Now. Who might you be?" There was an even mixture of kindness and tension in his voice.

"Ada Picou," Ada answered, "And this here is Adelle," Ada gestured to the girl. Ada paused, then added, "Durand, and Zeke," she tilted her head at the man she had ridden in with.

"Yes, yes, I know yer names. Who the hell are you all though and why are you out here in the God forsaken land?" Lewis asked with the impatient frustration of an elderly man.

Ada nodded and sighed lightly. "Well, ya see, ah'm trailing a bounty. Man we mentioned earlier. He rode through this a way."

Lewis nodded, his eyes narrowing.

Ada hardened her jaw and resigned herself. "Ah'm from Louisiana and ah've been on the hunt fer a spell." She tipped her hand to Peachie, "Ah found this here girl in Nebraska, alone—"

"We are following my little brother. He was taken by the man that killed my parents," Peachie broke in to tell her own tale.

As Peachie spoke Ada saw Lewis's eyes soften at the plight of the young girl. He shifted his weight and looked at Peachie, "I'm right sorry miss. There was a fella here last night and he had a boy with him. The fella was all frocked in black and had sharp blue eyes, much like what you all describe. Appeared in the yard out there like a coiled viper."

"That the gunfire we heard?"

Lewis nodded. "He drew on me. I don't cotton to nobody's

barrel none. I didn't make it through the war to end up shot by some damn drifter," Lewis spat.

"Say what he wanted?" Ada asked the grizzled older man.

"To kill me, I expect. Didn't ask for nuthin'. Just drew on me," Lewis answered. He looked down at his thick and calloused hands. "I already had my rifle in hand as I was walking around the building." He sat still for a moment and worked his jaw. "I saw the boy after I fired. I reckon I'm glad I missed." He looked at Peachie. "If I'da seen the boy, I wouldn't of fired none." His eyes drifted to the rough and dry boards surrounding him.

"Ya fought for Jefferson?" Ada asked, shifting the subject.

Lewis nodded, his attention drifting to a time in the distant past. "I did, long damn time ago it was. Feels that way at least."

Ada felt a connection with the old soldier. "My pa, he did also —" Ada halted when she noticed the gray of the man's wool trousers.

Lewis noticed Ada's gaze. "I didn't desert none, fore you ask," he spat, his eyes offering a challenge. "Got myself wounded and discharged. They found me bloody in the belly of a field surrounded by the corpses of my regiment." The air around Lewis grew heavy with old miseries and memories. His voice was low and rough as he continued, "Lost me a few fingers and toes to boot." He shrugged. "But I kept most of my parts."

Ada's tense attitude softened a bit as she thought back to her father.

Lewis turned his attention to the quiet Peachie. "Where you from? Not Louisiana, no? Like her?" he gestured to Ada.

Peachie shook her head. "I lived a ways outside of Paris when I was small. My parents brought me and my brother to America. They wanted a new life and better for us." The pain was evident upon her face, and Lewis did not press the girl for more and fidgeted awkwardly as Peachie's eyes became watery.

Ada watched the conversation, knowing how hard it is to remember when you did not want to.

Lewis turned to Ezekiel and pursed his lips. "You, sir, need a bath."

"You could use the same, sir," Ezekiel said.

Ada and Peachie each gave a half-hearted chuckle.

A moment of silence descended upon them before Ezekiel turned to Peachie. "What was his name?"

"Who?" Peachie responded with a curious tone.

Ada shot Ezekiel a look full of daggers, but he kept on talking.

"Your Pappy. What was his name?"

Peachie wiped at her damp face as she answered, "My parents' names are Antoine and Marie." She spoke softly, yet the pride in her voice could be heard by all.

Lewis pulled the worn hat from his head and his thick, scarred fingers played nervously upon it. "This ain't no place for ya ma'am, if I may," he said. The old soldier's voice dripped with sadness. He continued addressing Peachie, "Yer here for your brother?"

Peachie nodded.

Ada, still listening quietly to the conversation between the haggard old man and fresh young girl, spied another pale lizard as it darted by the open door.

"Miss Picou has been hired to rescue my brother," Peachie said.

"What the hell?" Ada jumped. Her full attention back on the conversation, she questioned, "Hired? Who'n the hell hired me?"

Peachie sat primly. "I just decided I did," she answered coolly.

Lewis chuckled at the look of consternation on Ada's weathered face.

"What're ya pay'n me with?" Ada asked indignantly.

Peachie pulled out a small key from on a chain around her neck. "My brother has one too. I have money. It's in a bank in New York. Do you think my parents would travel with everything that they owned?" As she spoke, she pulled a piece of paper out of a small gap in her hemline and handed it to Ada.

Ada slowly took the paper as if it would sting her and read the small print. "Damn girl, ya do have funds seems."

"They are—were—smart people, my parents. . ." Peachie's voice trailed off as she thought back to her parents buried on the road behind them.

Ada nodded curtly. Her lips pursed as she passed the banknote back to Peachie. "Alright then. Seems ah'm working fer ya kid," she said as her eyes wandered to the dust as it drifted through the light.

The group sat in the building and shared old tales after that. Lewis talked the most and shared vivid details of his military service as a sharpshooter and sniper, as well as about the family he left.

"She thought me dead," Lewis said in a low a dead tone. "She went and married a friend of mine in town who had come back 'fore I could get word to her," he said. Lewis hung his head low. "My children, they don't know me none. Just some sort of bedtime story I imagine."

Peachie looked at the old soldier. "Why don't you go home?"

He shook his head and looked out the doorway into the gloaming. "War, killin' men. . . I'm not who I was when I left home," has said in a low voice. "I may as well have died. Better I'm a story than something. . ." he held his hands up, ". . . like this."

Ada thought about her father and remembered the ways he

had changed by the time he came home from the war.

Lewis eventually shook off the weight of the old memories and turned his attention to Ada. "Blue eyes like ice."

Ada met his eyes wrapped in wrinkles and recalled her own memories of the Preacher. Shenodded.

"I know to strike a snake 'fore he strikes you," Lewis said, his voice drifting as he spoke.

Ada gnawed a bite of some of the dried meat she had packed from the last time Peachie made a kill.

"He had a smile that split his face, but it didn't go near his eyes." The old soldier shuddered.

Ada listened intently, knowing that the description fit the Preacher all too well.

As Lewis detailed the encounter, Ada looked at Peachie. The girl was also listening, absorbing every word with bated breath. Ada chewed her lip while thinking about the evil man and her worry for Henri grew.

The blood drained from Lewis's face as his tale unfolded. "I didn't see the boy, I assure ya." He shifted his weight in the bedding, making the boxes and boards below him creak and crack.

Peachie tilted her head to him and her lips formed a thin smile in an attempt to reassure him.

Lewis blinked his eyes, which were sharp with anxiety. "My gun was ready and my instincts kicked in." The old man's voice trailed off. "He asked for water after our altercation. Kept his hands up," Lewis said.

Ada's eyes tightened. "Must be desperate, seein' as you already fired upon him."

Lewis shrugged and nodded. "Must be. That or insane. I tried to talk to the boy, and the fella told me he was a mute."

Peachie spoke up, "Henri is not a mute. He speaks well for his age and is learning his letters."

Ada set her jaw as her mind made another connection between her brother and Peachie's. "Too much like Arden," she mumbled to herself.

Lewis became terse. "I could tell something weren't right, so I said so." A shiver struck the man as he continued talking about the Preacher. "Man turned on me and had a long knife drawn." Lewis's faced turned red. "I stumbled back and fell over the threshold." He sighed and rubbed at his neck. "Lost grip of my gun when the stock slipped by the hinge of the door and I fired wild." He pointed to a hole in the wall above Ada's head.

"Yer lucky to get two shots off and live," Ada observed skeptically.

The rough and surly man wiped his face. "So, yer sayin' what I was told weren't true?" Lewis shifted again, "I'm telling you now," he said as he looked at Ada with a wildness in his eyes, "I didn't know who y'all were."

Ada shook her head and grimaced. "You were on that rye." Ada pointed to a case of whiskey peeking out from under the bedding.

Lewis's face turned dark, and he balled his fists.

Ada met his challenging look and adjusted her weight while slightly tensing her muscles. "That's why you shot at him when he rode up on ya, ain't it? It's also why ya missed twice, even though you're one hell of a shooter," she pronounced.

Lewis fumed, but soon deflated, his chest sagging as his arms dropped. The old soldier could not stay angry when he looked at the little girl from France and nodded in embarrassment.

"What happened then?" asked Ezekiel.

Lewis started, having forgotten about the other man for a moment. "Well, the gun went off. Didn't hit nuthin," Lewis answered quickly as Ada took another bite of dried meat. "When I went back out, they was long gone." He gestured with his hand to the doorway.

The four sat in the darkening room and waited for the night air to cool them as they contemplated all they had heard from each other.

"You all can sleep here," Lewis offered. "Ain't much, but it is a roof. I got some old meds to trade for the mutton. Here, girl," Lewis said as he tossed Peachie a knife. "This is mine from the war. In case that old Union rifle jams on ya." He smiled softly to the girl as she took the knife and thanked him with a gentle nod.

"Alright, we'll take ya up on the shelter," Ada stated as she slid over to lean against a crate and lowered her Stetson.

Ezekiel and Peachie shared a quick look and Lewis nodded at both of them as he rested on his back atop the bedding. Peachie curled up by Ada, and Ezekiel stretched out on the small area still covered by the porch.

"Thank ya, Lewis," Ada said from under her hat.

The night was long and the only sounds were the occasional chuffing of the horse and mule.

In the morning light, Ada eyed the ground afresh for tracks. What she found told her of a single horse headed south without deviation.

"Dammit. He's leadin' us on," she grumbled as she made her hands into fists and looked over the land. Ada cursed and shook her head in frustration. Her plan to stay out of the Preacher's wake was foiled repeatedly by his actions. She thought she could ride around and past him in order to get to the ranch and William before he did, but that seemed unlikely now.

The old soldier walked over to Ada and commented, "He might be lookin' to bushwhack you."

Ada shook her head, pushing away her thoughts about William. She tossed a rock to further let out her frustrations. "Nah, that devil wants to do worse."

"Where is he leading y'all?" Lewis asked.

Ada chewed on the answer for a moment before she answered. "He is headin' to my ranch and the man ah got there."

The old soldier stood looking at Ada for a while before he turned back to the small building. He spat, stood straight, and adjusted his belt, "I'm coming with y'all."

Ada shook her head. "Ain't no damn way, ya old coot. This ain't no pleasure ride. This man here is a damned killer. Ah've already got enough with the kid and the straggler. Ain't no way another person is going to slow me up," she ranted out her troubles.

Lewis narrowed his eyes. "I'm a damn good shot and I got a mule. I won't slow ya down and you might find a need for a retired sniper," Lewis said with confidence.

A stern young voice came from the shed door and announced, "I am hiring him as well, Miss Picou. Lewis is coming. He has his own guns and knows how to use them. Plus, he has his mule that he can ride with Zeke."

Ada sighed in consternation and threw another rock into the distance. "Like a damn circus." She looked at Peachie and, after taking a few strides toward the girl, turned back and stomped over to her horse.

Showdown

CHAPTER ELEVEN

Ada cinched the girth a second time after letting the horse breathe out his air.

"You seen sumthin'?" Lewis asked Ada, as he gestured to her shaking hands and gave her a knowing look.

She turned and walked back to the building, ignoring him. She favored one leg over the other, the pain in her hip flaring up.

"Shot too?" Lewis asked.

Ada turned around to glare at Lewis and met his eyes. "Caught two bullets outside the Badlands. No more questions," Ada said as she turned away.

The old soldier shook his head as he looked back toward the building. "Too cold for me there."

"She said, 'it was a 'freezing hell' out there'," Peachie offered.

"I ain't never been that far north," Lewis said as he carried a saddlebag to the mule.

Ada listened to the three's chatter as her mind wandered to the Dakota Territory, and a shiver hit her. "Was it the cold or the Preacher?" Ada grumbled to herself. She considered for a moment their intertwined lives from her childhood as her fingers flexed and her knuckles tightened. She took a moment and checked her guns. Rolling the bullets in their chambers gave her a small comfort.

"Was it that man with the boy?" Lewis continued.

"Damnit, ah said no more questions," Ada shot back to the old man as she stomped over to her horse.

Ezekiel turned to the soldier. "She been at him a while as far as I heard tell."

Peachie also helped explain based on all Ada had revealed to her. "Been her whole life. That man killed her parents and her brother—"

Ada cleared her throat, and she stood ready with the roan. "Y'all worse than hens," Ada barked as she stepped into the saddle. "Ya got a question, keep 'em to yer damn self." She looked around and took in the landscape. She noted that the surrounding grass was thinner and hardier than what she had ridden through not many days past. Rocks stood out in the soil and the land rolled before her as the blue sky dusted with clouds like sifted flower meandered slowly from east to west above.

Before they left the ramshackle building completely behind, Lewis dug out an old pair of boots from a rotten crate and tossed them to Ada. "A peace offering," he said.

Ada accepted the boots and saw they were worn and old, with heels that slung low. She tipped her hat to the old soldier in thanks and checked the bandages on her foot before slipping on the boots. Nothing was infected and the wounds from the wolf attack were healing well thanks to Ada's diligence in keeping the bites clean and packed with moss.

"We need to move," Lewis issued orders as he fell back into his military mindset.

Ada pulled Peachie up onto the red roan while Lewis got on the mule himself, before helping Ezekiel step into the saddle.

"Damn man, you smell something awful," Lewis observed.

Ezekiel shrugged. "Drop me in a river if you see one."

"Happily," Lewis answered.

The southern wind died down as the group prepared to leave.

"You oiled my leathers?" Ada asked Peachie.

"Yes, I used the last of it," the girl said, looking worried.

"Much obliged." Ada gave Peachie an appreciative look pregnant with unspoken meaning.

"Wait!" Peachie leapt off the roan and walked off to shut the gate of the paddock. "Gotta leave it like you found it," Peachie said and nodded in satisfaction.

"Yer gonna be alright. I kin feel it," Ada said as she sat hunched over the saddle horn for Peachie to finish her business.

Ezekiel had collected and sorted the foodstuffs and supplies

Ada had brought with her from the trading post and added to their shared collection what Lewis had amassed at the shack. There was still mutton and foraged vegetables, which meant that the food would serve their group for a bit as they crossed the country. Meanwhile, Lewis checked his assortment of rounds and his weapons, taking accurate stock of the inventory and how it would serve them against the man they hunted. Ada with had her six shooters and Peachie with her rifle were ready as they would ever be as they refilled their water skins and canteens at the trough by the paddock.

Even the animals were anxious to be on their way as they pawed at the ground and tossed their tails, tuned to the electricity in the air as they were.

Ada thought about the previous night and deduced that the group had settled into a sense of safety and calm from being together. Ada figured that it was probably good to travel in a group like this, even though it was not her way. Still, it may serve her purpose yet. Extra eyes allowed each to let down their guard, maybe get much needed sleep, and hopefully avoid an ambush.

The four rode away from the shelter and into the wake of danger cut by the Preacher. With Lewis and Ezekiel atop the shaggy-haired mule while Ada and Peachie rode the roan, they traveled easier.

The air was comfortable, and the day was overcast. A gentle breeze nudged the riders from behind and the only deviation in the landscape was the occasional river birch or black locust tree.

It was a calm and uneventful ride for some time as they made their way westward. At some point, Peachie fell asleep, leaning against Ada as the afternoon came and went. To Ada, the girl looked small and wane. The stern authority that Peachie occasionally presented was gone and left behind only a small thing. A soft breeze pushed Peachie's hair around her crown and Ada could feel the soft strands on her own neck. Peachie's was just another youthful innocence that was destroyed by an evil man.

Ada bit her jaw and gazed up at the clouds as a distant roll of thunder peeled from the north and bolted past them.

That night, they silently made camp in a small hollow. The land had calmed them, giving them each time to ponder something different.

Ada's mind was bent on the Preacher and William. Peachie worried over the fate of her brother. Ezekiel had a single-minded focus on caring for the shaggy mule while occasionally muttering Jebediah's name. Lewis set to work on the coffee and meat as he fell back into his military training.

Once all was said and done, Peachie crawled into Ada's arms just as she did the first night they camped. Ada, set her head on the freshly oiled saddle, tilted her hat over her eyes and let rest come to her.

As she drifted off, Ada heard the men speaking in low and soft tones.

"They both look so peaceful," Ezekiel noted.

"Both of them, for now, look blissfully unaware of their situation," Lewis added sadly.

Ada heard the gruff man turn on the ground as he settled into the spot where she assumed he found sleep. Ada peeked at Ezekiel through one slit eyelid and found the man sitting with his back to a gentle rise in the soil where, after a few minutes, his soft snores filled the darkness. Ada wondered if he dreamed of Jebediah, as she often dreamed of those she too had lost, as she drifted off.

Waves of heat shimmered under the warm and pale-yellow sun. A powdery blue sky held up by hard and brown earth surrounded the travelers. The small group moved at a steady pace set by the mule, though was still faster than when Ezekiel traveled by foot as Ada and Peachie rode slowly upon the red roan.

"Good boy," Ada said, as she patted the roan and gave him time to graze along their route as they made their steady way after the Preacher.

The mule seemed, over time, to become less than happy to leave his shelter for the wild. He constantly nipped at Ezekiel, making the man whine and howl with his displeasure. Even when not being ridden, the mule had to be watched to keep him from bullying the man.

"He's after me, I knows it," Ezekiel stated earnestly after a particularly nasty bite on his finger from the mule.

"Nah, he's smiling. He likes ya," Ada jokingly observed.

"I know better than that." Lewis laughed. "Probably just need a bath. He doesn't like your smell no more than I do."

Even Peachie giggled, her mind momentarily distracted from her worry.

Ezekiel grumbled curses as he sucked on his wounded finger.

"Weren't my place no matter," Lewis tossed his head back in the direction of the cabin. "Zeke, we got a long walk ahead of us."

"Yes, sir. Yes, sir we do," Ezekiel said, finally taking his finger from his mouth. His head bobbed in further agreement.

The soldier took on a stern but gentle tone. "Zeke, ya can't drag yer ass none."

Ezekiel nodded more seriously as he considered the mule. "I'll do better. Won't let him get the best of me."

The red roan's tail swished in the air as he walked steadily and slowly while the mule followed with his head down.

"Are those buildings?" Peachie suddenly blurted out and pointed far ahead of them as a line of black dots emerged on the horizon. Her eyes were far better than the adults and she almost always noticed things before anyone else. There was an ominous look to the blackness ahead that, to Ada, looked like tombstones in the distance.

Ada nodded. "Looks to be. Let's head in, see if we can stir up anything for our hunt." Ada's eyes were screwed up and her face was frozen with a look of concentration and focused intent.

"We could use some real food," Lewis said, breaking her concentration.

Ezekiel silently nodded and had an obvious yearning look upon his face.

"Jerky and wild carrots can only hold us for so long," Peachie added.

Ada sighed at the many comments and complaints. "Ain't nuthin' wrong with jerk."

The travelers continued on for a time in silence as they waited for Ada's final decision.

"Well, he knows we're trailin' him," Ada spoke her thoughts out loud as she resigned herself to the visit.

A stoic silence of dread sat upon the group as they worried about what they would cross in town.

Peachie squinted into the distance, straining her keen eyes for any sign of her brother. "He's alright, isn't he?"

Ada nodded, knowing that the truth was that the boy was safe as long as he could be used to bait her.

Peachie worried her lip.

"Ma said that was a bad habit," Ada said, as a flood of memories hit Ada in the gut. "Told me my lip'd fall off." She paused and looked into the distance. "My brother, Arden, he used to crack his knuckles."

Lewis and Ezekiel listened in silence, their faces fringed in sadness.

"He used to crack everything else too," Ada added. "Used to drive Ma plum mad," she said.

Peachie listened quietly as she slid her hand over Ada's on the horn.

"Henri picks at his fingers. Our mother says he will get infections," Peachie mumbled.

Ada sat quietly in thought. "Yer ma sounds smart."

Peachie nodded proudly. "In France, she taught children. She was like a governess going from home to home," Peachie stated, with longing in her voice.

Ada's eyebrows drew together. "I know 'bout teachers, but what's a gov'ness?"

"She cared for other children in large homes. She taught them their numbers and letters. We did not have a school building, so mother traveled," Peachie said, frowning. "She stayed with them often."

Quiet rode alongside them for another mile, yet Ada could tell

Peachie was still itching to ask something.

"What ya about? Ah ain't yer governess or nuthin." The woman muttered to herself under her breath. "Ah ain't nobody's nanny."

"Eh, what's wrong Ada?" Lewis spoke up from behind them. "Ya seem like a good nanny to me," he snickered.

Ada waved him away with a look of disgust on her face.

As they rode onward, they paused occasionally to let the animals graze.

"Like being in a snare," Ada said, while thinking of the Preacher.

Ada gnashed her teeth in frustration, and Peachie worried her lip in fear. Ezekiel and Lewis waited nervously for the women to make sense to them.

The sun was setting and, by the time they could make out the different buildings of the town, lights peeked from windows in a way that presented nothing foreboding in their visage.

"Looks inviting," Lewis observed. "Can't wait for some real vittles." He rubbed his hands together and smacked his lips.

Ada was about to speak when a threatening howl pierced the evening stillness.

"Wolves," Ezekiel said as he cast his eyes around in the darkness.

CHAPTER TWELVE

"Wolves," Peachie's voice was tight and laced with fear.

Ada nodded and, sitting high in her saddle, scanned the area for movement as Lewis brought the mule to stand by Ada's horse. The mule he shied into the side of the roan, his fear palpable. The group struggled with whether it was the right choice after all to not set up camp and instead ride straight for the town.

Ezekiel had stepped out of the saddle and stood nearby, rubbing at his leg. "Got an old wolf scar, these darn wool trousers scratch at it awful," Ezekiel said. "That howlin' makes it worse."

Ada threw him an Arkansas toothpick that stuck in the ground at his feet. "Ya still ain't gittin' no gun from me," she stated.

He nodded, clenched his jaw, and shifted his feet into a fighting stance with his weight on the balls of his feet, bent knees, and straightened his back.

Ada raised an eyebrow and tilted her head, curious to see whether whatever Ezekiel could do would really be effective against a pack of wolves.

"They sound close." Peachie's teeth chattered softly and jostled her words. The girl's eyes were wide and her head turned left and right as if it were on a swivel. Peachie had already saved Ada from a close call with a wolf, and Ada knew the young girl would be anxious.

A sliver of a moon crept into the sky and reflected off the barrels of the group's raised guns. Ada drew her Colt and stepped out of the saddle While Lewis got down and stood across the mule from her. Even Peachie had her rifle out and braced against her shoulder as she looked down the ladder.

All around them were shadows that leaped throughout the landscape. The howling had raised everyone's hackles and everyone's nerves, already raw, reached a fever pitch as a small pack of wolves slunk into view.

Ada narrowed her eyes and held her gun at the ready. What seemed like countless growling and snapping jaws descended upon the travelers as the wolves closed in on their intended victims.

Peachie, quick to pull the trigger, squeezed off a shot and sunk a bullet into the earth just past one of the pack. Just as Lewis was about to fire himself at what he guessed was the leader, the thundering of hooves broke the focus of the wild canines.

All eyes shot in the direction of the tumultuous sound to see a group of horsemen from the town running the wolves away. In a flash, the blazing brightness of gunfire illuminated the night and wolfish yelping followed.

The party of four squared up with muscles ready and eyes narrowed as six riders wrapped in dust stopped short of Ada.

"Follow us!" The man in the lead gestured with his pistol in the direction of the town.

Ada, Peachie, Lewis, and Ezekiel shared concerned glances.

Lewis cast a measuring eye over the men and said, "Let's do as he says." He then took the mule and followed the riders with his gun still drawn and ready for anything.

Ezekiel trailed him on foot and yelled, "Come along, Ada!" Ezekiel nervously waved the large knife at her over his head.

Ada and Peachie shared another look before Peachie nodded.

The next moment, Ada was back in the saddle and thundering after the men.

"We have a wolf problem," the sheriff stated as he sat on the desk in his station. His left leg was bandaged and dry drops of blood flecked the dusty floor around him.

Ezekiel nervously fingered the edge of the blade he carried and Lewis scratched at his whiskers absently as the two stood near the doorway and appeared unsure whether to be inside or out. Peachie meanwhile sat with her back straight in a chair by the desk as Ada stood with arms crossed and listened patiently.

"You all are welcome to stay over at the Brass Buckle Inn. Be wary on the street and don't leave town unarmed," said the sheriff.

Ada nodded and looked at Peachie before she asked about the

Preacher. "Has a man in black riding with a boy been through here?"

The sheriff thought for a moment and shook his head before looking out the window. "I can't rightly say. We get a number of odd folk 'round here. There's a bounty on them wolves and the pelts go for a high dollar back east. Some fellas come in all in black and some got kids with 'em. This here town used to be a junction and was bustling before the wolves became aggressive," the sheriff answered.

Ada's disappointment showed in her dropped face and sagging shoulders as the conversation turned to the town's troubles and away from her own.

Once the Sheriff was satisfied that the travelers were properly informed, the group cautiously crossed over to the stables and set the horse and mule up for the night and paid two armed stable hands were given extra coin for brushing and alfalfa. They then entered the Brass Buckle Inn, doubling as a bar, where a silent player piano stood in a corner in a reminder of better times.

Ada's eyes swept the room quickly. The few patrons sat hunched and silent and were casting furtive glances toward the street. She set Peachie up with some food at a nearby table, the girl's gaze wandering, focusing on nothing.

Ezekiel, Lewis, and Ada leaned against the old bar drinking rye while deciding their next course of action.

Lewis leaned over to Ada and said, "We can't save these

folks."

Ada's free hand traveled over the worn wood. She hadn't been at a real bar since she left her ranch in the New Mexico Territory. Being inside of one again like this one reminded her of home. The smooth old grooves and gloss met her warmly. Instead of glass or a mirror behind the bottles, there was shiny tin. It caught the light and reflected through the vessels, giving her something to look at as she considered the location of the Preacher.

"Did he pass through here?" Ada quietly said to herself. They had lost his trail not long after leaving Lewis's small building, and the town sheriff offered no new leads.

"Even if he were, he ain't here now," Ezekiel pointed out.

"We was right on him. Must of gone 'round the town," Ada said with a sneer. "Sure wish ah'd stumble upon him. Ain't nuthin' more ah want to do than end his sorry ass," she said while biting back bile.

"Maybe the wolves run him off," Lewis speculated. Ada frowned, not quite agreeing, but said nothing to the contrast as Lewis went on, "Might be stuck for a bit. No telling when we will be able to slip off."

Ezekiel nodded as he sipped on his drink. "Already been bit once by them wolves. They tore ma leg up sumthin bad."

Ada sucked her teeth and turned to lean her back against the bar.

"*Merde*," Ada cursed as she downed her shot. She twirled the glass in her hand and furrowed her brow. "Can't stay here. We can't him slip us none. This ain't our fight—"

"Ever since they ran off them bison the wolves have been going after us," the barkeep sighed.

Lewis nodded in understanding. "Probably the army trying to git the natives to scoot."

"Yessir," the barkeep said as he slid plates of cooked greens and pork across the bar.

"Much obliged." Ada took up her plate and sat by Peachie who had already finished eating.

Ezekiel and Lewis took up together at a nearby table, the worn chairs dragging heavily on the dry wood as the weary travelers settled in.

"We can't stay," Peachie said, while looking desperately at Ada.

"Nah, we ridin' out soon as we can," Ada answered. She looked out the window as she chewed her food, barely tasting the meal. "Ain't too many folks on the street," she said, noting the empty road.

"It's them wolves," Ezekiel worriedly surmised.

Lewis shook his head and ate his food while quietly grumbling to himself between bites.

"Whatcha fussin' 'bout old timer?" Ada pressed the man.

"Well, nothing. I got a job to do," he answered.

"Well, if'n you hadn't been hired none. What in the hell else you be doin?" Ada's harsh tone was even more grating now after failing to gather any leads regarding the whereabouts of the Preacher.

"I've found something to occupy me. Don't you worry none," Lewis said while meeting Ada's gaze. "Right now, there ain't nowhere I'd rather be than right here beside that girl. You got it in your gut as well as I do. 'Fore you were even hired you had her in tow," he snapped back at Ada before turning back to his meal.

They decided to stay the night upstairs at the Brass Buckle Inn. Ada and Lewis, heavily armed, checked on the animals before turning in.

"Nothing getting past us," one of the stable hands said proudly.

Ada threw another coin to the men. "Better not. Ya'll shoot 'em a lot?"

One man looked at the other and said, "About one every other night. But they are getting wise about us being here. Been going over to the other side of town. Mr. Harper used to camp in the church and used to take shots at the wolves, but he got hisself tore up bad," the stable hand shook his head.

"Runs the general store and keeps us stocked with supplies these days," the other stable hand continued. "Folks stop by and try their luck, but lately the stage and the strangers have been keeping their distance. Rumors get to flying about and this old town starts to look less and less like an opportunity and more like a curse."

Ada looked down the street and past the inn until she made out the faint outline of the church.

"Nobody goes there now, too dangerous," one of the stables hands answered Ada's unspoken question.

Lewis nodded and threw a bag of ground coffee to one of the men and the stable hand's face lit up.

"Thank you, sir, said the one who caught the bag."

"Yes, thank you much," the other man spoke up.

Ada and Peachie shared a small room at the inn while Lewis and Ezekiel took up residence across the hall. Every other room was empty for lack of other travelers in town.

"You think this town's cursed?" Ezekiel started.

Lewis shook his head. "Nah. Ain't no such thing. Folks just get funny ideas in their heads. I seen it happen in the war. Men would get to thinkin' sumthin' on 'em was lucky 'til it weren't." Lewis sat in a small wooden chair near the window and started cleaning his rifle. He glanced out the window while preparing his tools. "There is a bounty on them and the hides sell," Lewis quoted the sheriff.

"We could use the money. I want a fresh start somewhere,"

Ezekiel said thoughtfully. "I been running since I can remember. Somewhere out there gotta be a place I can settle, but I just can't picture it is all. . ." he trailed off before picking up again. "How you hunt wolves, anyway?"

"All we gotta do is hit the alpha," Lewis stated.

Ezekiel shook his head. "What's that?"

"Leader'a the pack," Lewis answered. "Like a commanding officer. Those soldiers'll either scatter without him, or they'll fall in the dirt alongside him."

Ezekiel shook his head in confusion and handed Lewis some gun oil. "This is a spooky town," he whispered.

Lewis nodded and set himself to going through his cartridges.

By the time the howling started just outside of town, Lewis was already in position within the church. It was late in the night and the street was long since silent, while the lights in the buildings were put out and nothing moved but the cottonwoods fluttering their leaves in a casual breeze.

The church was old and poorly built, leaving it with a slight lean to one side that would only progress as the years passed. Lewis stood his extra shells up on one of the few flat surfaces to keep them from rolling away to be lost among the rows of pews coated in a thick layer of dust. The pulpit was grimy with a matching layer of filth, and the few windows were thick and dingy with an oily film that obscured his view.

Lewis pried the window up and, thanks to the building's lean, the window held its position.

The old sharpshooting soldier settled into a position that overlooked the main street and the outskirts of the buildings. There were no sounds in the night, just the quiet movement of black velvet shadows that danced furtively in the darkness.

Lewis squinted while trying to pierce the night with his gaze and locate his quarry. The scent of the pork he had pocketed from his dinner to use as bait set out carried on the wind. The meat sat under a scraggly and sad excuse for a bush in the front of the church.

The sounds of padded feet were faint, yet reached Lewis's ear. On a silent night like this, any new sound stood out. He calmly watched the stalking predators from his high position and waited for his chance as four wolves crept close to the church.

As the wolves approached, a larger animal emerged from the night and snarled and snapped at the four smaller canines.

Lewis quietly cocked his gun and leveled his iron sights. As he waited, more wolves made their way onto the street. Soon, an entire pack filled the area around the buildings like a herd of cattle. The largest wolf was now close to the church and to Lewis. Lewis could see the scars on the massive muscular body of the one creature capable of controlling a pack of this size and felt a slight hint of respect for the fierce beast as he readied his shot.

Just as he was about the pull the trigger, gunfire erupted from the balcony of the inn across the street. Lewis firmly pulled the trigger and fired into the wolves, the barrel of his rifle bumping up slightly from his surprise.

The next moment, the large and scarred wolf lay dead, with a bloody hole placed squarely in his head. Lewis stole a glance up to see the street was alight with gunfire and, illuminated by the blasts, he made out Ada, Peachie, and Ezekiel.

Wolves fell in the street on all sides. Most scrambled to escape, and many of those failed.

Lewis saw the sheriff outside on the planked decking in front of his jailhouse, firing with wild abandon into the massive pack of wolves. Outside the general store was yet another man brandishing a shotgun.

The night was raucous with gunfire and peppered with the smell of black powder and blood. There was a human scream in the distance and Lewis soon spotted a deputy fighting back the snapping maw of a large black animal. The man's screams faded and were lost to the wind as the sheriff shot the wolf to save his deputy. . . but it was too late.

The remaining wolves eventually scattered, but not without leaving numerous corpses littering the roadway. Down the street, people were peering from doors and windows as the sounds of gunfire died down. An incredibly heavy silence followed the uproar.

The wolves gone, Ada yelled across the way to Lewis, "Enjoy yer pork!"

Lewis watched the unfathomable woman from Louisiana go back into the inn with a grin on his face. He chuckled and sat with his back to the wall where he dozed off to the smells of religion and gunpowder with a slight smile upon his face.

The following day, Ada, Peachie, Ezekiel, and Lewis worked together to skin the dead animals.

Peachie refused to dress the wolves, but she did her best and helped drag the bodies to villagers that could. She also kept the scavengers at bay. "We're not eating those are we?" Peachie asked.

Ada shook her head. "Jist a bit, we got stock. Most of the meat will go to the general store." She patted her stuffed saddle bags.

"That'll be Mr. Harper." Lewis pointed to the man cleaning his shotgun just outside the general store.

While the travelers and townspeople cleaned up after the night's carnage, the sheriff had buried his deputy. He walked wearily over to where Ada, Lewis, and Ezekiel were cleaning the animal hides. "Good play there," he congratulated them. "We appreciate what you all have done."

Lewis nodded and sat up straight. "Ada, we can't carry all these hides nowhere."

Ada nodded. "We'll sell what we can here and leave the rest with the tanner. Y'all got a tanner, don't ya?" Ada asked the sheriff.

"We do, he is laid up right now though. He was attacked by those wolves a few days ago trying to skin one's hide." The sheriff sighed louder the more he thought of their few wins among the many losses.

"Why ya'll never did nuthin' like that before? Get 'em trapped like that?" Ada asked.

"Well," he spat some chaw, "We only got a few guns in town. We don't have the numbers," the sheriff answered as he looked to Lewis. "We don't have no soldiers neither. I saw what you did there. We could use a man like you around here, if you had half a mind of stayin' in a sorry place like this."

Lewis shook his head. "Appreciate the offer, but I got a job to see through first. I may come riding back 'round this a way though yet."

"Just me and Harper can shoot worth a damn left with my deputy gone," the sheriff sighed.

"What about them in the stable?" Ada said.

"Those two boys in the stable are green. Haven't shot a wolf yet," the sheriff answered.

Ada threw Lewis an incredulous look. "They said they shot a few a week," she stated.

The sheriff turned red. "No ma'am. They just bang around and scare them off is all. Neither one can shoot straight. Would be a waste of bullets."

Ada pursed her lips and thought of the hellfire those stable hands would have faced if her horse had been injured.

"Me neither," piped up Ezekiel. "I don't think I hit one of them big dogs none," he said sadly.

Ada gave Ezekiel a sidelong look. "Peachie is good with huntin' game, but that was something else."

"I tried," Peachie spoke up as she dragged another scrawny wolf to join the lessening pile.

The sheriff looked over the dead wolves and rubbed at his head. "I think we may shake the curse yet, thanks to y'all." He thanked the travelers before carrying on to check in with the townsfolk and confirm all that had gone on the previous night.

Ada tilted her marbled Stetson after the sheriff and went back to slicing a hide off of the wolf she was working.

Mr. Harper gave them a fair price for the hides and meat. Fairer, in fact, than would be normal in the face of such a glut in supply. In turn, they stocked up on supplies.

"Fresh coffee," Lewis said softly.

Peachie wrinkled her nose at the stuff.

"I got me a knife of my own now," Ezekiel said while brandishing a machete at Ada.

Ada frowned. "Put that damn thing away before you cut your hand off," Ada said before she walked to the stable. The rest followed behind her with now fully loaded sacks. "*Je vous emmerde!*" Ada cursed at the stable hands and they looked back at her with their eyes wide. "Ya sonsabitches told me ya'd protect my horse. Damn good thing he is alright. Ah'd done flayed you along with them wolves if'n y'all would'a let anythin' happen to him!" Ada spoke in a cutting voice that left no room for any reply.

Both boys hung their heads low and sheepishly helped saddle the otherwise well taken care of animals.

Ada tapped her spurless heels to the roan's sides and pointed him south. As they rode out of town, Ezekiel spoke up.

"Sure did like that town. My kinda folks." Ezekiel rubbed his belly and sighed as he recalled the good meal at the inn.

Lewis turned his eyes on Ezekiel. "Do you want to walk the rest of the day you jackass?"

Ezekiel started in surprise. "Well then, I guess I just won't say nuthin."

"Best thought you've had in a spell," said Lewis.

Peachie looked to Ada, who again sat low in the saddle, shaking her head as they journeyed anew into the bright and cloudless wilds.

Chapter Thirteen

They camped the next night on a wide-open prairie, leaving the comforts of the town many miles behind them. The horse and the mule were staked outside of the row of bedrolls and each had just enough lead to graze all night.

Ada watched Peachie rub down the animals with a burlap sack and instructed her in the best way to care for the creatures.

"I'll set a fire," Lewis offered after much of the other work was finished.

"Nah, ah got it," Ada said. "You keep an eye out for more wolves. Ah'm sure there is more of 'em 'round. Ya turnt out to be a damn good shot," Ada said in a confiding manner.

"You did alright yourself, Miss Ada," Lewis offered.

Ada shrugged. "Ah hit a few, but not nearly as many as you did. Glad yer ridin' with us."

Lewis set himself apart from the group on a small knoll, his rifle loaded and ready as a distant howl pierced the dark night.

"I got carrots," piped up Ezekiel. He smiled broadly and held a sack aloft as Ada prepped the fire and readied to make some coffee.

Lewis looked at Ezekiel skeptically and called out, "Where you get that from?"

"Along the road," Ezekiel gestured back toward the town.

"That's someone's farm back there," Peachie said in surprise. She admonished the man with a wag of her finger.

"Ah, don't be sour on him none. We got sumthin' extra to eat." Ada took the sack and looked inside. "Carrots, alright." Ada nodded before she tossed the sack to Peachie. "How 'bout a stew?"

Peachie shook her head and frowned over the idea of using stolen vegetables. "We don't have enough water right now."

The entire group's minds circled around thoughts of hearty stew as they all went back to setting up their camp for the night.

During the night, Ada heard a rumbling moving in from the east. It was too dark to see, but she recognized it as the sound of many hooves. She sat up and saw Peachie's eyes glinting in the low light of the fire.

"A herd of sumthin," Ada whispered to the young girl.

Ezekiel and Lewis propped themselves up on their elbows, no longer sleeping through the growing din.

"What's that?" Ezekiel whispered.

Ada shook her head in the half-darkness. "Cattle. And a lot of 'em, judgin' by the racket."

Lewis nodded to no one but himself.

Deep and resonant the hooves made the ground itself tremble beneath Ada. The sound made her think of her ranch with William. While she had been living with him, they had amassed a small herd that was intended to secure their future livelihood. She wondered how the herd fared now and if their hooves ever thundered so loud as the ones currently approaching.

The mule stepped nervously around his picket. Meanwhile, the roan was calm, so accustomed to the wilds as he was as the sound, low and rolling, grew and grew until it drowned out every other noise.

Slowly the four travelers stood and took what they had previously laid out up into their arms. They cautiously moved to the horse and the mule.

"Ah miss that sound," Ada said while attempting to project her voice, yet keep it barely discernible above the noise. "Big enough herds about." She looked around to get her bearings and, while the sun didn't yet lighten the sky, she already knew her direction.

Peachie was tense and sat white -knuckled, gripping her bedroll onwith one hand and the big red roan with her other.

"They comin' west, it seems. Must be free range. Somebody'll be 'round to herd em come time," Ada observed.

Soon the sound became truly overwhelming. The land churned and heaved under the travelers in slow rolls and each spoke softly to the horse and mule to keep them from spooking, comforting their own nerves in the process.

Ada patted the horse and spoke gently to him about their home in New Mexico. At one point, she thought she could hear Lewis talking to the mule about Georgia.

"You remember her, don't ya. . . ? Her wilds and curves. . . the way she smelled like home. . . she enjoyed every damn season and I wish we was still with her. . ."

Lewis spoke with a longing in his voice and a sweetness of tone Ada had not heard from him before. She eventually wondered if Lewis was talking about the state or a woman.

The air gradually became thick with dust and each of the riders covered their face as best they could. Their views of each other obscured despite how close they were. Ada and Lewis pulled up handkerchiefs they had procured from Mr. Harper in the town, Peachie pressed her face into her bedroll trying to hide from the strangeness of the night. Ezekiel tied his blanket around his head.

Lewis called over, "Zeke, you look like a damn bee hive."

Ezekiel shrugged.

A gentle, a storm with no rain thundered covered and rocked them. Occasionally they heard a huff of breath or the bray from a calf. Ada looped a Maggie rope between the two animals, securing them to one another and could hear Ezekiel praying at intervals in a quiet and low voice when she drew near to him.

"Suns up," Lewis said.

Peachie shook her head in disbelief as she peered through slit eyes. "It is?" She could see nothing through all the dust.

"Too much dust ta see anythin' though," Lewis added.

Peachie buried her face into Ada's chest as fear took hold of the young girl. "Will this ever end?"

Ada held her tightly in one arm, the other braced on the rope and her horse's mane as wind gusted in from the south and pushed some of the dust away to finally reveal their group's surroundings.

Peachie peered out of the dirty folds of Ada's long-handled button down and gazed speechlessly upon a massive and black herd of cattle moved around them.

"Damn," Ada whispered, her voice muffled by the dust-choked handkerchief.

Ezekiel made the sign of the cross, and Lewis flanked opposite the mule's thick neck in an attempt to give the beast some comfort.

Through dirt-caked eyelids, Ada watched the massive herd pass them by. They had made camp in a little depression that gave them some protection from the north wind and, apparently, the herd's direct path thanks to how the terrain directed the cattle around the small piece of land due to a large gray rock that cut the herd like Moses might part a sea of fur, muscle, and horn.

Ada shook her head and wondered at their luck that came and went whenever it pleased.

Another two hours passed until eventually the last of the herd made its way west, the north wind soon clearing the view in their dusty wake. The ground around the travelers was turned over every which way and loose soil over a mile wide marked the path the herd traveled.

Lewis pulled at his handkerchief, now thick with dirt, and spat out a wad of brown muck. "Lord, I'll be diggin' dirt outta my craw fer years," the old man fussed.

Ada, Peachie, and Ezekiel all chuckled, relief washing over them.

Peachie looked at the horse and mule, both brown with dirt and chuffing and braying in discomfort, and frowned. "We need a river."

"Yeah, they ain't been this dirty, well ever prolly," observed Ada as she and Peachie knocked the dust from their bodies and checked over their belongings. The saddles were untouched, albeit filthy with settled dust, and pressed up against the protruding land.

"My carrots are all gone," Ezekiel observed sadly.

They cinched up the girths and saddles of the horse and mule As Lewis worked the loose dust out of his rifle's barrel.

"Shouldn't a drawn," Lewis said with a defeated sigh as he tapped his gun. "Gonna be hell to clean."

Ada nodded and looked over the land. "Yeah, ah'm sure there be a lot of cleanin' at the next waterin' hole." Ada shifted their heading slightly south of the herd's wake. "Hope they wasn't runnin' from nuthin' that scared 'em off."

The travelers immediately scanned the horizon for wolves that they did not see. Only a pale blue sky and burning late morning light met their worried looks.

"Brush." Peachie pointed to the west.

"Might be water nearby," offered Lewis.

Ada nodded while untying and separating the two animals. She pulled at the reins to steer the roan and gestured with her head. "Let's see what that's about there."

The extra dust and grime seemed to weigh upon them and slowed their ride. There was a thick coating of dirt on all of their clothes, keeping them stiff and scratchy.

The travelers eventually came upon a small creek with wide glides and pools at the meandering edges. The water was cold and moved with a calm serenity that lacked any urgency. Both the horse and mule were brought into the creek and the animals responded eagerly to the bath, the mule nearly pushing Ezekiel into the water as the travelers worked together to rub down the animals with wet burlap sacks first.

"Careful round the eyes and ears, Zeke," Ada called.

Ezekiel waved back in understanding and grumbled at the mule.

"Can't have any sick horse and mule," Ada mumbled to herself. "Don't let 'em wallow either! In and out. Waters too cold."

Ezekiel waved her away with his free hand and shot back, "I knows that firsthand!"

Once the animals were taken care of, each of the group took a turn downriver to wade in and remove the filth from themselves as best they could.

Ezekiel came back from over the bank first, saying, "I think I got dust in me."

Lewis laughed, "Ya prolly did ya dern greenhorn!"

Peachie's brow furrowed as she tried to puzzle Ezekiel out. She scrubbed at her clothes in the water around her and turned the clear water brown with the dirt she washed off.

"Jist keep them floaters away from tha water," Ada fussed as she rubbed down the saddles.

Lewis chuckled as he cleaned his guns. "I dug a hole like my pappy showed me."

Ada shook her head at Ezekiel and then responded to Lewis, "Good fella, yer pappy."

Peachie washed everyone's bedding in the creek when she finished cleaning her own clothes.

Ada, finished with the tack, found a tall greasewood. "I got some twine here," she said as she took out a small ball of twine..

Peachie watched in confusion as Ada stripped a branch and tied some string to it.

Ada winked at the girl. "Fishin' time, girl."

Luck, it turned out, was again on their side. By the time the sun set, Ezekiel was roasting four fish on green branches over a fire that night.

"Ain't much," Ada said, "but at least it ain't wolf or snake." The woman chuckled wryly at Peachie's expression as the girl struggled to hold the fish with her greasy fingers. Ada tossed her a small carving knife. "Cut it up, ya don't want none of them small bones to stick in ya."

Peachie nodded her thanks and used the knife to cut up the small pieces of the fish.

"You ain't too bad a cook," Lewis complimented Ezekiel with a mild mixture of surprise and admiration playing on the old soldier's face.

"My pa, he showed me how to roast em." Ezekiel's eyes drifted eastward.

Ada recognized the furtive look in his eyes and knew what it was to miss home. The group sat in silence, exhaustion washing over them.

The food long eaten, Ada sat on an old log at the water's edge when Peachie walked up to her.

"You think he came through here?" Peachie inquired.

Ada tilted her head a bit. "Prolly." She let her eyes wander across the slowly moving stream and then down to the soft mud at the water's edge. Ada found comfort in looking at the dark mud of the bank as her mind drifted to the swamps of her childhood.

CHAPTER FOURTEEN

Peachie wiped the knife off in the water she had used while eating and the big red horse wickered when he saw the girl doing so.

Ada caught a smile play across the young girl's face and thought about herself at that age. Peachie was just a bit younger than herself when she had lost her family. Ada's chest tightened, and she felt a sharp pain in her side from where the Preacher had shot her.

Peachie walked over to the hobbled horse and rubbed her hand over and under his soft muzzle. He lipped at her hand and she let out an involuntary giggle.

It was one of the few times that Ada had seen the young girl relax so thoroughly. "Walk him a bit, if ya want," Ada offered.

Peachie, unaware she was being watched, blanched lightly before nodding and quickly untying the horse's legs.

Ada gestured in a circle with her finger. "Then rub him down good with dry grass."

Peachie nodded at Ada's instructions and took the red roan's lead. It was the first time Ada had given Peachie the sole responsibility for the big horse. "You look really tired boy," Peachie spoke gently to him as she issued her care.

"We got corn in one of them sacks," Ada added in a half-distracted lisp. She cursed under her breath as she stared off at nothing.

Ezekiel walked over and sat by the saddles with a can of lard he had melted over the fire and slowly rubbed the oil into the recently washed leather.

Once brewed, Lewis served Ada a tin of strong black coffee as she painfully limped toward the small fire for a cup, all of the pains and aches she had before wolves and the cattle returning with a vengeance. Lewis watched her closely as she moved around the camp, but said nothing.

Ezekiel met Lewis's eyes, then Peachie's. They all wore worried expressions as they busied themselves, not wanting to earn Ada's ire with their stares.

Ada sat heavily upon the ground by the dug-out fire pit with tin cup in her hand. She became lost in deep thought regarding the Preacher as she sipped the hot drink. The group gave Ada her space and said nothing, nor did they bother her with questions, and she appreciated the calm quietness as she settled her mind.

As the darkness crept in, Peachie finally asked what they all were avoiding:

"What happened to your leg?"

The woman looked the girl in the eye and smiled weakly. "Ah caught a bullet." She looked over and saw Lewis and Ezekiel's eyes on her, too. "Well, ah guess y'all need to know a little more about that bastard," she began as she recounted the tale of her chase through the Dakota Territory. As she told her story of the frozen land, Lewis slapped his leg.

"Damn, I ain't never been that far north. Sounds terrible as all get out," Lewis said.

"Yeah, it was. Ain't nuthin' quite like it," Ada said, holding her cup in both hands while watching the steam floating up into her face. When Ada had finished telling them about her hunt for the Preacher in the snow, the travelers shared beans, Arbuckel's, and silence.

Night unfolded and a thick veil of darkness slipped over the camp. Ada noted that Peachie was sleeping, Ezekiel snored, also asleep, and Lewis was staring into the embers of the fire with a sad and distant expression upon his face. Ada dozed on and off, unable to still her mind after the activities of the past few days, the Preacher weighing heaviest upon her thoughts. She was both exhausted and jumpy at the same time.

"Ya ever been shot?" Ada asked Lewis.

"No. Seen it a bunch, and I been stabbed twice with little knives," he answered. "My arm never did heal right and it's angry in the winter."

Ada added, "Bet it hates Yankees too."

Lewis smiled at her quip. His mirth faded quickly as he thought back about the war. Lewis threw a few dry twigs on the smoldering ashes and teased out a small, hissing flame. Lewis glanced toward the dozing red roan and leaned against a small cottonwood. "You got a blood feud with that man?" Lewis asked.

"Yea, sumthin' like that," Ada answered flatly.

"He musta wronged you something strong to ride all over the Dakotas looking for him," Lewis observed.

"Ah'd been huntin' him fer years. Crossed many state lines looking for his sorry hide—" Ada began. Whenever the Preacher came up, once Ada started talking, she always found she could never stop. "Rode out of Louisiana and up the coast. Spent a few years in the Appalachians and then scooted over to the Ozarks. He was always ahead of me. Cut my teeth on bounties till ah knew what was what." Ada shook her head as she remembered those days. "Lost his scent and thought he musta died on the trail. Rode herd for a spell, weren't too bad at it. Ended up in the New Mexico Territory and staked a claim with a few head of cattle." Ada found herself confiding more in the old soldier than she had anyone other than William.

Lewis cleared his throat. "You ride in Georgia ever?" The muscles around his eyes stayed tight with restrained memory.

Ada noticed Ezekiel was no longer snoring and, when she peered over at the girl, she saw the flames reflected in Peachie's open eyes. "Yea, I rode them hills, too. Spent time south of Atlanta, Barn-something," Ada tried to recall. "It's been a spell," she concluded.

At the mention of Georgia, Lewis spat out his chaw into the

sizzling fire. After a flurry of curses, he stated, "That damned son of a motherless whore." He punched the ground a few times to punctuate his exclamations.

Ada raised an eyebrow in confusion.

"Damn that son of a whore Sherman. Shoulda hung him fer what he did," Lewis said with a low, grumbling fury.

Ada nodded, understanding setting in as she thought of the war her father had served in.

Ezekiel spoke up, "That's a bad fella."

"That bastard!" Lewis continued cursing General Sherman with a flurry of colorful language that ranged from "shit eat'n carp" to "bloodless bastard cur," with some curses made up on the spot that made even Peachie grew pink with embarrassment.

Ada was surprised by the soldier's language. She watched him with her eyebrows raised, appreciating the distraction from her own troubles. After giving him time to let off steam, Ada spoke up, "Alright now, that'll do." She tilted her head to Peachie and red crept up Lewis's neck.

"I'm sorry Ms. Peachie, I-I don't know what come over me." Lewis wrung his hands for a moment and fidgeted in place on the ground, his hard attitude softening before the young girl's innocent eyes.

"It's okay, Mr. Buchanan," Peachie said as she put her hand on his knee. "I know you were in the war."

Her kindness and gentle nature struck them all, and everyone in the company turned away in an effort to hide their wet eyes from each other.

Peachie spoke kindly, "My father used to get to talking in that manner whenever my mother would talk about France." Peachie looked toward the small fire and, sitting back, removed her hand from the old man's knee.

Lewis, uncomfortable with having the girl's focus on him any longer, shifted the conversation back to Ada. "Whatcha trap up there in the snow? I'm guessing you ran traps?"

Ada sighed. "Ah mostly trapped beaver when ah could find 'em. Any of the small and soft pelts sold well up there at the fort. Folks back east don't seem too particular. Heard tell some of it went overseas. Got no proof of that, though."

"Where you learn that?" Ezekiel asked.

"I ran across a trapper up there, big fella," Ada said. "Just watched him and learned. Ah spent a long time alone and learned everything ah needed here and there."

Peachie spoke up, "Do you have any children, Ada?"

Ada shook her head. "Lawd no." was her flat answer. "Ah don't have no husband neither, 'fore ya ask."

Lewis chuckled, and Peachie frowned at Ada.

Ada adjusted her hat, sliding it over her face. Laying back and putting her head on the clean saddle, she said, "Ah ain't got nuthin' else to say 'bout that." Ada stated, putting an end to the conversation for the night.

Chapter Fifteen

Ada started the day with her body creaking and cracking with her every move, along with a splitting headache. She found her limp was worse due to the events of the past few days.

"Still bothering you?" Lewis gestured to Ada's leg.

"Yeah well, ah did git shot," she shrugged. "Beats bein' dead, ah suppose," she mumbled As she stood tall and stretched. "We gotta fella to kill."

"Sounds like he is overdue for his postin' and we're the ones to carry it out," Lewis said.

Ada nodded. "We'll see to that."

With a final belt buckled, both the roan and the mule were saddled to ride. "All done here," said Ezekiel.

Ada nodded to him. " Yer a good fella, Zeke. Ah'm glad yer around."

A great big smile spread across Ezekiel's face at Ada's rare compliment as he helped Peachie step up into the saddle.

The four companions left the creek behind when it veered east at a bend. Canteens and water skins full, they braced themselves for the trek into further unknown territory as the hours turned into days and they made their way following the sun.

"How far is New Mexico?" Peachie asked.

"Far enough," Ada sighed. "But we're making make'n alright time. We will ride until we see the mountains and hang a left southbound thar."

The cool air had nearly faded away altogether thanks to the wind that came in from the south bringing a dry warmth that made Ada all the more eager to reach the end of their trail. Although the roan could've easily sped up, the mule set their group's pace as it sauntered along with Lewis and Ezekiel in tow.

"What's that sound?" Ada turned to Lewis.

"I dunno," Lewis shrugged. "Zeke, I think."

Ezekiel held up a small bag that made a strange noise. "My sack of teeth," he said proudly.

"What?" Peachie gawked.

"I got a bag of wolf teeth from that town." Ezekiel shook the bag and flashed a gap-toothed smile.

"Ya can't put them in yer mouth, Zeke. They don't fit like that," Ada stated.

Ezekiel nodded. "I knows that. Just got 'em maybe to make somethin' with, or somethin' like that. Maybe I'll trade 'em to an Arapahoe fer somthin' like some beads."

Lewis chuckled at the strange, scraggly man.

Seeing no other travelers or farmers on their route for some time, the sudden appearance of a town on the horizon startled the travelers.

"Ah reckon we should skirt this one," Ada suggested.

"We may need supplies," Lewis offered brusquely.

"Alright soldier, ya might be right. We ain't in New Mexico jist yet," Ada begrudgingly agreed. "Might also be able to git some news on the man we're trailin' and see if he's been through," Ada said.

Between the group and the town stood a small grove of short junipers that cast some much-appreciated dark shade.

"Let's git there and come up with sumthin' to do next." Ada gestured with her head to the trees and led with her roan, the donkey naturally tailing without fuss as the two animals made their way to the shade in the hopes of catching some rest.

Lewis pulled the mule up alongside Ada and the roan. "We still got a long ride ahead, but I don't want no more trouble. I'm damn near done with civilization." He spat at the ground as he cast a narrow eye toward the false-faced buildings ahead. "That last town with them wolves done wore me out. Ain't as spry as I once was."

"Ah am in a similar spot, Lewis," Ada said. "Ah don't want none of anybody right now 'cept that damn Preacher."

Lewis looked at Ada for a moment and rolled a smoke. "What you plannin' now, girl? It ain't easy to kill nobody, even the bad ones," he added with a knowing look.

"Got no choice in the matter," Ada spoke in a low voice and with her eyes pointing south. "He gotta die, no two ways about it. My brother, Pa, and my Ma. . . they deserve that. Not sure how it'll go, but ah got my guns at the ready," Ada said.

"You've got enough of them dead men on that horse," Lewis added while eyeing the bulging pack of shells Ada carried.

"Well, ah ain't gonna be caught flat-footed again," she said.

Peachie stepped off the horse when they pulled up to the trees. Lewis eased off the mule and Ezekiel followed.

"Gettin slow thar, old timer," Ada stated dryly as she swung her right boot over the haunch of the roan. She jumped down and hit the ground harder than she expected, dropping to her knee. Her face was pained and tight as she braced herself with her hand on the horse's leg.

"You don't look so good yourself, lass," Lewis said as he threw Ada a shrewd look.

Ada cursed the pain lancing her thigh and pulled herself up, using the stirrup. "Damn no-account leg," Ada grumbled as she steadied herself.

Lewis cast a subtle worried glance Ada's way. "I know wounds. You want me to look at it?"

Ada shook her head. "Nah, it's long closed up. Just puckered now. Landed wrong is all," Ada explained.

Peachie turned the roan and walked him away from Ada.

"She's doin real well," Lewis observed, changing the subject to something more comfortable. "What of her folks?"

"Dead. Found em a ways north of ya," Ada said.

"Yer man?"

Ada nodded. "Same way as my folks. Ah couldn't leave her out there, found her by luck." Ada paused for a moment before continuing, "Or maybe she found me."

Lewis sat on a large rock and slipped a cigarette between his lips. "Ya doin the right thing, girl."

Ada looked at him with a sardonic scowl. "Ain't been called a girl in a spell. Haven't felt like nuthin' but anger in a long damn time."

"Yeah, life'll do that to you after a while."

Ezekiel slowly walked over and set their bags under a juniper. "Smells good here,"

The trees were shy of twenty feet tall at their highest, and berries dusted with a powdery purple had started to swell on the branches. The grasses around the group swayed gently in the southern breeze as the hobbled horse and mule stood together, taking in their fill.

Peachie sat by Lewis on the ground and began rubbing oil into the two saddles.

"Got a little prodigy there." Lewis gestured to Peachie with his head.

Ada shrugged in confusion, her eyes glancing at Peachie as she chewed her lip. "Don't know nuthin' bout no prodigy, or whatever, but the kid is good. She's a quick learner."

Peachie did not look up from her task, but smiled proudly as she worked.

Nestled between two trees, Ezekiel started a fire on a pile of sand and rocks.

Ada looked up. "Strange tree. . . being this close to a tree in a while has got me hankerin' fer the forest." She threw a suspicious eye over the horizon. "Ah don't much care for these wide-open places. No cover, no dens, not a perch. . ." Ada trailed off while thinking of the Preacher.

"The Colorado Territory got great forests, and I heard tell of a wilderness of sorts in New Mexico. Northern part of it, at least," Lewis tried to comfort Ada.

She shrugged and gave him a weak smile. "Ah've heard stories of the Rockies. Ah aim to see what's true and what's not. At some point," Ada mumbled as she drew a line in the loose dirt by the fire.

An uncomfortable silence followed.

"Good spot Zeke," Lewis eventually spouted. "Tree will diffuse the smoke."

Ezekiel nodded. "My pa showed me. Jebediah said my pa was smart. . . except when he let me be off with my brother." Ezekiel shook his head.

After settling in, the group rummaged through their saddlebags and pulled out an assortment of salted meats and a few sweet potatoes.

"We won't make it," Peachie said while looking at the food a worried expression.

Ada looked back at the rolling prairie. "Might scare up a rabbit or such if we need to."

"Why don't we jist shoot us a bison?" Ezekiel offered.

Peachie nodded upon thinking of all the meat one giant buffalo would give them. "I agr—"

Lewis shook his head. "We don't have the ammo to waste and that is too much meat to carry. Besides, didn't you hear that old sheriff? He said them wolves went at the town because there was no game to be had," he grumbled. "No, we'll make do and figure something else."

"Ah ain't killin' somethin ah can't use all of," Ada chimed in.

Lewis nodded and thought out loud, "We'd need a bigger rifle, then a small wagon to carry everything off." He shook his head again as he went through all the logistics of taking down and dealing with such a large animal.

Peachie looked at the ground and tapped her foot. "We'll go to town then. See if there is news on my brother and I'll buy us what we need. I have money. Ada has pelts to trade also."

Ada nodded skeptically, "Ah *had* pelts. Sold and traded everything back at the town with them wolves. 'Sides that, where you got money on you?"

Peachie pulled out the banknote. "I know about getting a wire. I've heard my father talk about it," she said.

Ada shook her head as she tried to figure the girl out.

Ada chewed her lip as she cast a worried look toward the town small town. The distance of the junipers to the town was under four miles as far as Ada could size it up, and there were two streets that intersected perpendicularly at one end. Ada could barely make out the row of false-faced buildings that flanked the main street and could faintly make out the row of buildings where it ended. "Don't look like much of a town from here. Looks more like a couple of rows of trouble," Ada stated coolly. "Won't have much far as supplies out here in the sticks neither. Might have some news though," she added as she mulled things over.

"Just need some basic rations and maybe a couple bottles of busthead. They're sure to have that," Lewis said eagerly.

Ada grimaced sourly at the old man. "Damn sharp old man."

She tilted her head back to look at the sun and, taking her Stetson off, wiped the sweat from her forehead as she thought about their prospects with the town.

"What if he is there?" Peachie asked the question everyone was thinking.

Ada turned to Peachie and answered flatly with cool eyes, "Then he'll die there."

"I'll go," Ezekiel spoke up.

"Tha hell ya will," Ada snapped.

"He won't recognize me. That fella talked to Jeb," Ezekiel said. In a low voice, he added, "I hid."

Lewis sighed as he looked Ezekiel over. "I'll cut his hair and fresh'n up his look some."

"Ah should go. If he's there, ah'll get the drop on him," Ada said, adjusting her belt. "

No, please let Ezekiel go," Peachie pleaded.

"Why's that?" Ada asked.

"Zeke and I can go. I'll pretend to be his daughter. If we see anything, we'll come back!" The girl tied her hair in a bandanna and unfolded a hat taken from the bottom of a small bag.

"What's that?" asked Lewis, indicating to the unusual hat.
"This is my father's beret. I took it, when—" Peachie's voice

cut off. "I'm going," Peachie said.

"Nah, ya ain't. Ya stay put here. No need to put yerself in no danger," replied Ada as she limped over to the roan.

The group watched her with bated breath as the horse sidestepped Ada and continued grazing.

"Damn it then!" Ada huffed. She was as exhausted as was the horse.

"We are not far away. You can keep an eye on us from here," Peachie offered as she took Lewis's rifle over to Ada.

Ada shifted her weight and looked Peachie and Ezekiel over. "Alright Lewis, do what can with this one. Y'all just be careful. Git in and git out. Don't ask 'round too much and don't cross nobody," Ada said all this while unrolling a small wad of bills from her belt. "Take this. No need to wire nuthin. It ain't much, but it's enough for a few basics. See if they got a length of rope. Ah need new rope," Ada said.

Lewis nodded before walking Ezekiel over to the mule where he proceeded to clean the man up.

Ada used the scope on Lewis's rifle to look over the town. "Ah don't see his horse. But he could be hidin' it somewhere," she muttered while peering through the glass. "He knows we're behind him, so keep your wits about ya."

Peachie nodded as Ada handed the rifle back to Lewis.

"Alright, looks tame enough. Git on then," Ada ordered.

Peachie stood proudly with her chest out.

"Come along, Zeke," Lewis said. A moment later, Ezekiel walked out from behind the mule.

"Damn, Lewis! Ya sure can work miracles. Still smells as hell, though," Ada said.

Lewis smiled. "The clothes are mine. They're not perfect, but they'll do."

Peachie looked at the clean-shaven Ezekiel in wonder. "You look very different without a beard."

He smiled a crooked grin that looked all the more crooked now that he was cleaned up and blanched a tone. "Alright Miss Peachie, Imma ready," Ezekiel said as rubbed at his newly shorn face.

The two walked over to the mule and unhobbled him. Lewis consolidated their supplies and gave the empty bags, satchels, and sacks to Ezekiel who placed them behind Peachie across the shaggy gray mule's back.

"Don't let my mule get into no trouble," Lewis stated as he sat back against a stone protruding from the ground and stretched his legs out before him. He was dozing in the shade before Peachie and Ezekiel had ridden off.

"Ya sure y'all don't want me along?" Ada pressed.

Peachie shook her head. "No, thank you. You stand out a bit

too much and we want to be in and out without trouble."

"Ah ain't worried about ya, girl. It's *him* that's got me on edge." Ada scowled.

Peachie bit her lip before speaking. "Zeke will be alright. He is useful."

"I'm nice too," Ezekiel said to Ada with a smile and a wink.

Ada shook her head and frowned. "Yer crazy is what ya are," she pointed out.

Ezekiel smiled and gave a half-hearted shrug before leading the mule away westward to the small town.

Ada watched Peachie and Ezekiel make their slow way away from herself and Lewis. After they had covered two miles, Lewis woke from his nap to find Ada oiling her guns.

"Your leg is worse than you let on." Lewis said. It was statement, not a question.

She pursed her lips. "His horse ain't there. The girl needs experience. This'll do her good."

Lewis looked at Ada through narrowed eyes. "She already seems pretty grown to me. Small, but sort of wise I guess," he said. "You taken to her?"

Ada stopped her hands and set her gun down on the folded Arapaho blanket in front of her. "It's my damn fault her folks are dead and buried in an unmarked grave in the damn

Dakotas!" Ada gnashed her teeth as she spoke. "It's my fault her brother got took. He is doin' it to hurt me, to make me feel all the pain over again. He's *bordelation du diable!* There is somethin' evil in the man and he has been stalking me as much as ah've been huntin' him."

Lewis listened as Ada ranted on.

"Ah got to help the girl be ready for life like her folks woulda done. It ain't gonna be the same, but if ah can git her back to the town that was there fer me. And if they ain't hospitable, *je m'en fous*, some town 'round thatta way'll do. Well, that'd be a start fer sure," Ada said resolutely. "We ain't jist ridin' back to the New Mexico Territory fer me and fer William. That girl's gotta have her brother and they gotta have a place," Ada growled. Ada noticed Lewis staring at her hands and when she looked down Ada realized she had started to shake as she was speaking.

"You didn't kill those folks," Lewis eventually pointed out.

"Ah know it, but ah might as well have. He'd not done it if ah hadn't been tailin' him." Sadness dripped from Ada's voice.

The juniper shifted slightly in the breeze as Lewis filled his nostrils with a deep breath and let the air out slowly. "You lose anything else up in the Dakotas, besides your step?"

Ada gave an involuntary shudder as she thought back to the cold of that place. She spoke low and slowly, "Lost my spirit fer a spell. Thought ah'd lost my ranch too fer a bit. *Sacre tchu,* that Athena," Ada rambled as her mind wandered.

Lewis frowned, taking in every word even if he didn't fully understand Ada's history.

"She may be kickin' still fer all ah know. Traded her the title of the ranch for a broke down nag and that Spence the kid carries," Ada said.

Ada stared off into the distance, her mind lost in memories of that far-off north country.

"And you lose anyone up there?" Lewis asked cautiously.

"A few friends, ah think." Ada rested her back against her saddle and tilted her hat over her eyes, ending the conversation.

Lewis gave a small, dry chuckle. "You got funny ways Miss Picou, you sure do." Lewis rested his back against a juniper and tried to make sense of the strange leaves that grew above him.

Ada heard the heavy hooves before she looked up and saw the shaggy mule bouncing along faster than she'd ever seen it move before, with only Peachie in the saddle. There were full bags hanging from the sweating animal, but the mood given off by Peachie was not celebratory.

"Zeke was arrested!" Peachie yelled. The girl was flushed and disheveled after the rough ride from the town.

"Woah, what happened to Zeke?" Lewis jumped to his feet

and took the reins from the girl as she hopped down from the saddle.

Ada crossed the makeshift camp to Peachie. "Out with it girl," she ordered, her face frowning and stern.

"They have him in the stocks. People are cursing and yelling at him," Peachie was wild-eyed and there were beads of sweat on her brow and lip. She halted for a moment as a tear raced down her face. "The sheriff whipped him in the street."

Ada clenched her fists, and her jaw flexed. "*Futre*," Ada cursed.

Peachie trembled beside the angry woman, despite knowing Ada's anger wasn't directed at her.

Lewis cursed under his breath and spat, "son of a bitch."

Ada took a breath and asked, "What'd he do?"

After wiping her face with her sleeve, Peachie explained, "He stole from the back of a wagon."

"*Mede*, of all the damn fool things," Ada cursed, her shoulder sagging a bit as she tightened her gun belt. She looked at the buildings in the distance and weighed her options. "We gotta go," Ada commanded, despite Lewis already having long since begun to pack up camp. "Well?" Peachie asked desperately.

Ada poured water into her hat from a skin. "Drink up, boy. Got to ride."

The horse drank noisily from Ada's hat, half of every mouthful spilling back out. Lewis, following Ada's lead, offered some water to the haggard mule.

Ada shook the water skin out with her other hand. "Dry," she muttered. "We gonna need water soon."

"We can scout some out past the town," Lewis pointed west.

"Roll over the next few miles should turn up sumthin," Ada pointed west. She turned to Peachie and found the girl was stepping from foot to foot. "Ya didn't happen to git water, didja?"

The young girl shook her head and blinked up at Ada in confusion.

Ada sucked her teeth as she walked around the roan. Ada patted the speckled red horse and caught Peachie casting furtive glances back to the brown and gray wooden structures of the town.

"Can't do nuthin' fer him," Ada said in a low, sad voice. "They hang thieves and the sod busters got no heart," Ada hissed with a grim finality. She grimaced at her own words and thought back to her father who dreamed of being a farmer in Louisiana as a pang of guilt shot through her gut. "Nuthin' good grows in the swamp," Ada mumbled to herself. "Nnuthin' but rot and smut grass."

"You can't leave him there. He didn't do anything!" Peachie pleaded.

Ada chewed her lip and donned her dripping hat, allowing the last of the water to cool her. She squared at Peachie with one eyebrow arched. "Spill it. Ya ain't tellin' us all of it," Ada stated with one eye squinted at the girl.

"I saw some boys take sacks out the back of the wagon. A man was loading the store and he saw Zeke standing by the wagon when he noticed the missing food. He started yelling at Zeke," Peachie reported in an increasing hurry. "I said the boys shouldn't steal, but one of the boys threatened to beat me. . ." her voice trailed off.

Ada could see the interaction in her mind's eye and judged the girl's character as one that wouldn't tell lies.

"Then they saw Lewis's mule and asked where he got it, but he said it wasn't his," Peachie blurted.

Ada rolled her eyes at the ineptitude of the man.

Peachie looked at the ground and dragged her toe across the dirt as she spoke. "I was getting you coffee. I know I should not have left him, but I thought about the coffee after we had packed up. I know you favor it." Peachie's brow furrowed as she recalled the exchange. "They said he was a horse thief, too."

Ada took off her hat and wiped her brow. "Lord almighty, what a damned mess. He fer sure is getting hisself hanged now."

Peachie stood in silence while watching the older woman come to her decision. The young girl held her breath, only breathing when she saw the look change in Ada's eyes. A moment later, the roan was saddled and ready.

"Ah'll fetch the old cul," Ada finally said as she stepped into the saddle with her slightly over-sized unslung boots. "Throw me that Maggie rope—"she called to Lewis.

"I got you some new rope, Ada," Peachie stated.

"Alright, give me that too," Ada replied. "Y'all ride on, ah'll catch up." She gestured with her head to the west.

"You think you can get Zeke out of trouble alone?" Peachie asked.

"Ah can get him outta that town, but ah can't work those kinda miracles."

"We've got the supplies all here," Lewis patted his exhausted shaggy mule. "Git Zeke free or my mule here ain't got nuthin' to chew on," said Lewis.

The soldier smirked, but Ada still detected the touch of worry in his eyes.

Lewis gestured with his hand to Peachie before calling her over to the mule once she hitched her bag on her shoulders. "Ada," Lewis said, as he looked back at the fierce woman. "Be careful. Still got work to do."

Ada nodded. She patted the neck of her horse and said, "Let's go, boy." Ada clicked and pulled the reins, turning the roan toward the small town and leaving only a trail of dust and worry behind her.

Chapter Sixteen

Ada rode into town just as the sun was coming to a rest behind the false-faced buildings. A sign greeted her which read *Gillette Mines*, the base of which was marred with graffiti which read *Closed Forever*.

"Looks to be a town on hard times, boy. Zeke musta given these folks a bit of distraction." Ada clenched her jaw and braced herself for what she would see.

Only once did she glance back to where she left the others. She could still barely make out their dark silhouettes on a hillock thanks to the failing sunlight.

"Ya damn fool Zeke," Ada hissed, her words carried away on the wind. Ada thought about all the time she spent alone in the Dakota Territory the previous season as she rode her way deeper in to town. "Didn't need to worry over nobody," she grumbled in frustration as she looked over the dusty town. "Lonely though, right, boy?"

The roan nickered.

Ada arrived at an intersection at the opposite side of town where the main roads formed a large "T." A general store sat to Ada's right, and there was a saloon to the left of her where an off-key tune rattled out of the shabby building.

"Sounds like an old tune my Pa would sing. 'The Vacant Chair'

I think it was," Ada told the horse. She observed that there were not a great many structures in the town—many of them dilapidated—and the street was short. "Ain't more than a hundred yards, looks to be. This place seen better days," she mumbled under her breath as she observed the half-busted and sun-bleached signs hanging from their rusty chains. Ada knew she could not take on a town by herself to save Ezekiel and that the law was against her. Once a man was branded a horse thief, the noose was assured. "It ain't my time to be on no wanted poster," Ada stated as she briefly recalled the numerous posters she had collected bounties on over the years.

As Ada rode onward, she came across another split in the main road that went to the left and right at a church. She spotted the sheriff's office next to the church where Ezekiel was locked up in a stock on full display in the street. His bare arms and feet stuck through holes and his rump rested upon the dirt road. Ezekiel's head hung low on his chest behind the wood, only the crown of his head was visible. Ada only hoped the man was passed out from exhaustion and not already dead.

"*Merde*, Zeke, ya damn fool," Ada whispered. She scratched at her jaw and considered her options.

A heavy weight of time-wrought fatigue lay thick over the town. Buildings lining the streets were in disrepair and in various stages of neglect. Most of the town was clear of foot traffic as the sun set and there were scant animals. Ada spotted a drunk passed out in an alley and a mangy dog trying to steal the drunk's leather boot. A few cats darted about on their evening mousings, and thin horses with protruding ribs stood tethered to the H-braces outside the inn. The saloon however was raucous and busy.

"Probably got the whole town in there," Ada mused. She did her best not to look at Ezekiel so as not to arouse suspicions as the shadows lengthened across the town's roads and as the sun dipped behind the buildings.

Ada rode up to the sheriff's office, where a deputy soon stepped out onto the dry decking to meet her.

"What business you got here?" The deputy, a man easily in his fifties, asked in an unfriendly tone.

"Passing through, friend," Ada answered in a false congeniality. "Been riding a spell, parched. Where is y'all's watering hole?"

The deputy gestured to the noisy saloon down the road. "Figured you would have seen that over there," he added sarcastically, with a sardonic smirk.

Ada looked down at Ezekiel with a neutral expression and, finding him indeed asleep, inquired, "What this fella do?"

"Horse thief. Stole a girl's animal and tried to steal from our general store," the man answered curtly. "We don't tolerate neither."

Ada nodded and narrowed her eyes. "Ain't nuthin' worse than a horse thief," Ada stated.

The old deputy nodded in agreement and leaned against the door jamb, causing it to creak under his weight. "This scoundrel is hanging tomorrow." The deputy frowned at Ezekiel.

Ada nodded. "Fine work, deputy. Ahmma git me that drink now."

The deputy tipped his hat to Ada and went back into the office. As he passed through the door, Ada spotted two more men inside.

She tied her horse up far to the right of Ezekiel, knowing she needed to get those men away from the sheriff's office and Ezekiel. Sauntering over in the direction of the saloon, she paused by the stocks and looked at Ezekiel, his body limp and with dried blood on his face and shoulders, who reminded her of a fifty-pound sack of grain. Her brow furrowed in anger.

Ada silently promised Ezekiel she would release him soon as she walked down the old, worn street toward the stables.

Seeing no stable hand, Ada quietly led all the horses out the back of the building and into the adjacent field. "Heeyah, git y'all," she shooed them outside and away from the buildings. "This should help a bit too," Ada said, as she snuck over and untied the lean horses from the braces outside the saloon.

The hungry animals ran off as soon as they were loosed to join their brethren on the open land outside of town.

"Hope y'all find some good grazin' out thar," Ada said, as she wiped her brow in satisfaction.

 She then walked up the old and crooked steps of the saloon

and through the batwing doors. Ada pulled a stool with a cracked seat up to the drooping bar.

"What's your poison. . . ma'am," the bartender said suspiciously when he looked up and saw a lone woman at his bar.

Ada loudly slapped her coin on the bar and boisterously announced, "Rye."

The bartender's demeanor changed when he saw the money. "Don't get many women around these parts," he said.

Ada shrugged. "Ain't much to see round here," she said dryly.

He poured a shot and shrugged.

"Ahmma lookin' to collect a bounty 'round these parts. Y'all see a fella all in black with a kid in tow?" Ada asked the barkeep.

He looked up at the ceiling for a moment and shook his head. "Only stranger we seen lately was that thief out there," the man answered as he prepared to pour Ada's drink.

"Leave the bottle." Ada slapped more coin upon the bar and looked around the dark saloon.

There were what appeared to be a few old bachelors sitting around the saloon drinking away their worries. One game of cards was in play at a round table near the front of the building.

"Rough town," Ada commented while taking a shot of whiskey. The sun had only just set and everyone already seemed pickled to her eyes.

The bartender nodded. "Used to be something. Had a mine and all these fellas had work. Now, it's not much of nothing."

She gestured to the street. "Ya called that thing in the stock a 'thief,' but what that fella do?" Ada asked.

"Horse thief," the bartender answered lowly as he peered at Ada through tight eyes. "You with him?"

Ada shook her head and downed another shot. As Ada set the glass down again, she noticed the glint of the metal star on the vest of a gray-bearded man next to her. A mirthless smile cut her face as she saw her opportunity to cause a distraction.

Rising from the stool, Ada stepped over to the sheriff. Before he even seemed to notice her presence, Ada used all of her weight and shoved him into the table of card players.

Chaos erupted as the table crashed and cards flew into the air. Curses bolted around the room, with accusations flying from all corners.

The old sheriff shouted unintelligibly and stood, shaking his fist at Ada for barely a second before one of the card players spun the sheriff around, not realizing who he was picking a fight with, and punched a solid uppercut into his abdomen.

Another of the card players leaped at Ada, but she sidestepped the man's wild swing and her attacker struck a man just to her left instead.

"Damn you!" The man on the receiving end of the punch yelled, following his curses with a roundhouse past Ada to strike the man who had thrown the first punch.

Chairs and curses were soon being thrown around the shabby bar as the townies all brawled in an alcohol and despair-fueled frenzy that sent cCards, money, bottles, and glasses scattering across the room.

"Y'all been bored fer too damn long," Ada commented as the violence unfurled around her. I wasn't long before two surly men made a bead for her next.

Ada let fly a left and right, sending the first man to the floor. The second man ducked past the first and barreled into Ada, wrapping his arms around her torso. They flew past the bar and hit the wall with a solid thud.

Obviously drunk, the clumsy man was unable to completely overpower Ada, and she drove her elbow into the side of his head. He dropped, quick and heavy, to the ground. Ada darted out the back door past the barkeep, who desperately tried to stop the brawl before his establishment was completely destroyed, but only ended up knocked out himself.

Ada slipped down the street, creeping along in the darkness until the brawl was well behind her.

Glass shattered as someone threw a chair through a window of the saloon and, .hearing the ruckus, from the deputies ran out of the sheriff's office and left Ezekiel unguarded.

"At least they ain't shootin' each other," Ada observed in mild surprise. No sooner had she made the statement, a gunshot rang out in the building, and the din out of struggle came to a halt.

Ada snuck her way over to the red roan and found him right where she had left him tied up by the sheriff's office. "Anxious, huh boy?" Ada patted the large red horse before grabbing the Maggie rope and tying one end to the horn on her saddle. She quickly led the horse to Ezekiel. "Hold on now," Ada said, as she diligently tied the rope to the stocks. Ezekiel was still unconscious, Ada was barely able to make out the rise and fall of his chest.

As she saddled up and turned the horse, Ada heard the sound of men's voices shouting.
Ada silently apologized to the roan as put her heels to the horse and the animal bolted, tightening the tough rope and shattering the weather-beaten stocks into pieces.

Ezekiel flopped to the ground with arms and legs bloodied, his restraints busted into bits around him. He moaned, his head lolling about as he came around with terror and confusion filling his bleary eyes.

Ada hopped down and grabbed Ezekiel by the scruff of his neck. "Git yer head right."

Ezekiel met Ada's eyes and his features softened in understanding.

"Let's git from here," she hollered to Ezekiel over the rising commotion.

The convict froze, stupefied as noticed the men charging their way from the saloon. The old and gray-bearded sheriff pointed his gun at Ada—

A loud explosion suddenly rocked the town as a small cart in the center of the town between Ada and the saloon erupted in a flash of fire and wood. Flaming splinters flew in all directions, the deep thunder of the explosion ricocheting off the false-faced buildings and shredding the stillness of the air for a few seconds in such a way that several of the pursuing drunkards fell to the ground.

Ada quickly yanked Ezekiel onto the horse's croup behind her, the dazed man's arms and legs flailing and loose as she rode the roan hard for the edge of town. The galloping roan carried them swiftly away from the blaze and astonished men as Ezekiel yelled nonsense at the flames and the men behind them.

"What a hootenanny!" Ezekiel yelled and whooped at the stars above. Ada rode hard, keeping every ounce of her focus on the land before her as Ezekiel jostled around behind her. She kept pivoting her head to look behind her, glad to find there was no pursuit. Ada hoped that by setting the horses free, the angry men would be delayed long enough for the pair to completely evade them.

Still, Ada recognized she'd just broken a significant law and the sheriff and his deputies would likely be after her as soon as they were able.

Lewis and Peachie had ridden west, so Ada made her way north. After stopping just long enough for Ezekiel to right himself on the horse, the roan carried the two riders through groves of trees and across thin shallow streams. It was hard for Ada to ride north all night despite knowing her will was bent south toward her ranch and the Preacher.

After a few miles, Ada recognized the faint sounds of pursuit. The men of the town were not subtle, and a shot rang out behind Ada as she pulled the roan into a thick grove of burr oaks overflowing with dense underbrush.

A group of men riding hard on various lean horses filed past Ada and Ezekiel, believing themselves to still be tailing their targets.

Ezekiel shivered and whimpered in the darkness when he saw the glints on the men's weapons and the murder on their hot faces.

"Hush now," Ada said firmly. "Let em pass and we'll double back. Amateurs, the lot of 'em." Ada sat stock still, along with the red roan, concealing their presence completely with the help of the dark shadows.

Listening to the fading hooves as she waited for them to die off completely, Ada decided to ride out of the grove toward the southwest by going through the length of the dense foliage.

Just as Ada was about to move, one of the straggling riders stopped near the grove of trees.

"You sure they came this way, Douglas?" the tired rider

moaned.

"Yeah, they are probably riding up to Jamestown. Damn town is full of filth," answered another man.

The tired sound of emaciated hooves soon faded into the distance along with the rest.

Once Ada was sure the men would not spot them, she turned the horse deeper into the brush. The roan took Ada and Ezekiel in a southwest direction as a soft and steady rain began falling.

"Might leave tracks," Ada noted. "If it picks up a bit, we'll be alright. Everything'll git washed out," she reassured Ezekiel.

Ezekiel nodded. "Yeah," he quietly said from behind her as he lifted his head toward the cool rain and it washed the blood from his wounds.

"I got ya. Hold on now man," Lewis said as he worriedly helped Ezekiel slide off the tall horse. .

"What was that back there in that there town?" Ezekiel asked, wide-eyed as he stood and rubbed at his arms and legs.

"Well, ah found a few dry candles and lit 'em up," Ada answered and shrugged nonchalantly while looking around at the gully where they had met up.. "Ah got a knack for blowin' stuff up," she added with a wicked grin.

Everyone gave Ada a questioning look.

"Another time y'all," she stated.

"Yeah, but now you're made," Lewis said in a half-awed panic. "What if they put up posters of you around here? Worse, what if they call in the Pinkertons?" Lewis shot Ada a slew of questions.

"Damn Lew, ah couldn't let Zeke hang now, could ah? Ah know ah busted out a criminal," Ada said as she turned to Ezekiel. "Well, ya already was a criminal, wasn't ya?"

Ezekiel nodded. "I were. Makes no difference to me."

Lewis threw up his hands in frustration. "Dammit Ada, you can't get yerself killed! The girl needs you," Lewis gestured to Peachie who had been watching in silence.

"Ah know. They was all drunk as hell, 'cept that old barkeep. Not sure where he stood though," Ada said thoughtfully. "Got bigger things to ponder, though. Even if they do come a lookin' fer me, won't be before ah'm done killing that Preacher. Lew, don't ride me none, ah know my mind," Ada said with finality.

Peachie gave Ada a skeptical look as the girl waited for the adults to decide their next move.

Ada pointed to the distant range. "We'll hit that and then head south. Gotta be moving before sun up."

"I can make it Miss Ada." Ezekiel spoke up with false joviality.

Lewis tried to clean Ezekiel's wounds as he helped the man change clothes, both men wearing various expressions of pain.and Ada winced when she saw Ezekiel's bloody back for the first time since rescuing him. "Ya ride the mule with Lew, Peachie yer with me," Ada said.

The four traveling companions rode west, leaving Ezekiel's bloody rags buried with their signal fire.

"You okay?" Peachie asked Ada in a soft, concerned voice.

The older woman thought for a moment before answering, "Good as can be ah s'pose."

"Did anyone get hurt?" Peachie asked worriedly.

"Nah, nuthin' serious."

"Nobody was shot?" Peachie pressed Ada for specifics.

Ada shook her head. "Only the old sheriff drew and that seemed to only settle the saloon. Only person hurt over there was Zeke," Ada answered truthfully.

Peachie nodded and gripped the saddle swell under Ada's hand.

"Found out that man weren't there," Ada added.

Showdown

Peachie gave a slight shudder, and her shoulders drooped. The two swayed gently on the back of the large red roan as he following the setting sun as it sunk slowly in the deep blue sky.

CHAPTER SEVENTEEN

Ada looked back at the mule and was grateful that Peachie had bought the rope considering she had used her original length to bust Ezekiel free and lost it in the mad dash to escape. Peachie's rope was now being used to keep the unconscious Ezekiel on the gray shaggy mule, the reins limp on the mule's withers after having slipped from his slack hands.

"Will he be okay?" Peachie asked upon catching Ada's eye.

Ada nodded and pursed her lips. "Ah reckon so. Jist needs to rest and heal up," she answered.

Peachie bit her lip. "Are you sure nobody got hurt?"

Ada cocked an eyebrow.

"When you blew up. . . whatever it was," the young girl added.

Pursing her lips into a line, Ada answered, "That cart ah blew was small and only startled those men enough fer us to light a shuck outta there. Ah got 'em running to the saloon and then set sumthin off between them and us. Let the horses out as well."

A confused look passed over Peachie's face. "You got everyone into the saloon?"

Ada quietly scratched her head while contemplating her response. "Well, ah kicked at a hornet's nest is all," she finally said to the girl.

Peachie continued to wear a confused expression.

Ada glanced at the horizon behind them, not sure of what more to say.

There were no clouds of dust pursuing their group, but the damage had already been done. Ezekiel was seriously wounded and could not travel with any haste without risk to his life. Morale was low, undermined by the people of the town who had beaten him.

"Ain't got no tail at least, it seems." Ada chewed at her lip as she led the horse and mule to the foothills of the great Rockies.

Heat began to beat down upon the travelers as they made their way further south. They eventually came to a rest in a deep crevasse wrapped in the protruding veins of the mountains, a secluded place where the roan shuffled to a small watering hole as soon as Ada stepped down and let him have his head.

Asa tried to help Peachie down, but the younger girl pulled away. "What?" Ada cocked her brow at the girl.

"I can get off this horse without help," Peachie stated with a slightly haughty air.

Ada shrugged. "Alright then, do as you will." There was a hint of something sour in Ada's voice as the girl hopped out of the saddle on her own power.

Ada turned her attention to helping Ezekiel down instead while Lewis unpacked the mule.

Ezekiel limped a bit, but with Ada's help, he made it relatively easily to a spot on the ground. "Thank you, Ada," he said with a grateful nod. "You did a lot for me back there. They was going to hang me for sure even though I didn't do nothing," the wounded man said sadly.

"They was bored and drunk, looking for a scapegoat to forget their own troubles. Ya got in at the wrong time and stirred the wrong folk up. It weren't right what they done to ya," Ada said kindly. "Your good people, Zeke," she said as she helped clean the wounds on his back.

"That old sheriff whipped me right there in the street," Ezekiel recounted as Ada picked more of the dirt from his lacerated back.

Ada nodded quietly, listening without comment. Peachie and Lewis stared openly at the escaped convict with concern in their expressions.

"Peachie, ride over to that river we crossed and get some clay for Zeke's back," Ada said before the girl could unsaddle the horse.

"Oui- I mean, yes."

Ada smiled sadly and continued to clean Ezekiel's wounds.

"I got a horn of gunpowder if he needs anything cauterized," Lewis offered. "Nah, ah think the clay'll be fine since he's not bleeding no more. Thanks Lew," Ada answered.

Ezekiel flinched occasionally as Ada cleaned the dirt and small stones from his back. After she finished going over his back, Ada set herself to cleaning up his wrists and ankles.

"Sorry about them splinters, Zeke," Ada apologized.

"It's alright Miss Ada. They're worth being free of that contraption. I don't feel 'em none at all," Ezekiel said with an optimistic tone. "I'll be alright once I get some rest. Probably been through worse, just don't remember it all."

Peachie soon returned with a bag of wet river clay that she'd picked free of bugs, stones, or roots.

"Thank ya, girl," Ada said, as she took the sack and began applying the clay to Ezekiel's bloodied body.

Ezekiel shuddered and muttered as Ada worked, and Lewis watched on in curious silence as he set camp.

"After this sits fer a while, yer skin'll close up and you won't get no infections," Ada explained.

"He won't get no gangrene because of that mud?" Lewis asked.

"Clay," answered Peachie.

"Dakotas taught me about it up there in the snow," Ada said.

"That right? I knew a lot of soldiers that could a used that poultice," Lewis stated gruffly as he worked.

Ada nodded. "Yeah, could a saved a lot of lives and limbs." The road-weary travelers made their way slowly through the rough terrain of the Colorado Territory. The snow-capped mountains in the distance loomed ahead as the group set up camp one night.

Ada shivered as she put her eyes upon the snowy tops. "Damn."

"Are you unwell?" asked Peachie. There was concern upon her face as she looked up at Ada.

Stoking the fire, Ada looked again at the snow piled on the tops of the distant mountains. "Ah'm fine. Jist thinkin' how much ah hate snow." Ada recalled her winter trapped and hunted in the Dakota Territory during a time when she unwittingly found herself trying to solve murders while avoiding her own death.

"What were you up thata way fer?" Ezekiel said.

Ada clenched her jaw. "Huntin in the woods."

"Like elk or sumthin?"

Peachie gave Ezekiel a knowing look as she explained, "She was after the man that killed her family and my parents, Zeke."

"Oh, that Preacher fella we're after now." He nodded in

understanding.

Lewis spat into the fire, and Peachie nodded at Ezekiel.

Ada wondered how many habits the young girl from France was picking up from her. The woman from Louisiana was relieved when Ezekiel did not press her further, yet she still offered, "Earned this limp up there and damned well don't like the snow."

The convict turned to Lewis next, not wanting to press Ada too hard all at once. "Lewis, you got my letter?"

Lewis nodded and rummaged in a bag he had taken from the old mule. The soldier handed Ezekiel a worn envelope creased all over with numerous folds. "Here you are. I ain't readin' it to you," Lewis stated as he boiled water for coffee.

"Peachie can ya read English?" Ezekiel asked the girl as he foisted the letter toward her.

"Yes, Zeke, I can read," Peachie answered.

Ada's curiosity was piqued. "What's that all about a letter?"

"This here is a letter from my ma back in South Carolina," Ezekiel answered. "I carried it with me for years, kept it in the lining of my shoe. Gave it Lewis when I put on his old clothes," the man continued.

Ada could certainly see that it was an old letter from the way the pages were a slight yellow and had frayed at the corners as Peachie opened it in the firelight.

Lewis watched the flames lick at the small tin pitcher of coffee, the water slowly coming to a boil within.

Ezekiel looked sadly into Peachie's eyes. "I asked Jebediah and Lew to help, but they only looked at it and never would read it to me," Ezekiel said sadly. He sighed, "It seemed he could read it alright." Then Ezekiel shook his head. "I don't know," he said. The man scratched at his arm as Lewis grumbled unintelligibly under his breath.

Ada frowned. "Ya sure ya want to know what's in there?"

Ezekiel thought for a moment before nodding.

Peachie began reading:

M. Ezekiel,

> *My dear son, you are all I have left. Your pa caught the consumption, as did your brother.*
>
> *I fear I may have it as well. Please find your way home and care for me as I die. It is the least you can do after abandoning us.*
>
> *- Your mother, June*

Peachie looked grim as she read the letter aloud. "The date is more than five years ago," she added sadly.

Ezekiel hung his head low and his breath caught in sadness. "They're all dead. . . my family is all dead." He lifted his head and stared far off into the dark distance as his new reality set in.

Peachie looked to Ada for answers, or support, or something, but Ada offered nothing. Peachie walked over to the shattered man and handed him the letter. "I'm sorry, Zeke," Peachie put her small hand upon his shoulder. "Lewis and Jebediah were trying not to make you sad," the kind girl added.

Ada watched as the escaped prisoner wept in the arms of the young girl. Ada found herself unable to swallow and her chest tightened.

A cold wind rolled down the mountain and the horse and mule shivered in the breeze. The duo stopped grazing and glanced at the four people sitting around the fire.

The four travelers settled around the crackling fire and contemplated their many individual losses.
In the distance, they heard a lone coyote split the night air. The long wail rode the air and was answered from far to the west as the sound died out. The surrounding land had become dry and hard as they traveled, and rocks now jutted out from the landscape as though growing in some massive, odd garden. The grass was short and coarse, leaving only the strong to survive.

Ada passed around a freshly refilled water skin, hoping to soften the mood. The intentional silence was heavy and persisted with the group's deep sadness. Ezekiel leaned back to watch the stars as Ada lost herself in the small flickering flames. Peachie's eyes, meanwhile, drifted to each of the adults.

"Zeke, ah'm sorry about yer family," Peachie said, mimicking Ada's speech as she shifted uncomfortably.

A moment of quiet passed before Ada added, "All of us got loss."

Ezekiel wiped his face with his sleeve and nodded. "Yeah."

Peachie nodded as she slowly chewed on her salted wolf meat.

Lewis sat at the edge of the fire, lost in thought, and smoked a freshly rolled cigarette in silence.

Ada took a drink from her flask and passed it to Ezekiel.

"Thank you," Ezekiel said as he accepted the offering.

The smell of peppermint wafted to Ada as the stars traveled above their heads.

Nobody slept well that night.

CHAPTER EIGHTEEN

The day was new, the light sharp and welcoming. The ride to the New Mexico territory had been a rough one, but Ada, Peachie, Lewis, and Ezekiel finally saw the town familiar to Ada in the distance.

Ezekiel gave a small yelp when he spotted civilization.

"It's alright," Ada said to him in a soothing tone. "Ah'm nearly home." The words tasted strange in her mouth.

Peachie seemed startled, but said nothing as she looked from Ada to the town and back.

Lewis led the mule by the reins and readied his rifle.

"Y'all can stay at the inn. Ms. Peace's. Ah need to git to my ranch," Ada stated.

Lewis shook his head. "Not a good idea, Ada. No need to divide us. It'll make you an easier target."

Peachie clenched the horn. "Ada, you can't just leave me here. Henri needs me." The girl pleaded.

Ezekiel shrugged. "I don't want to be in no more towns Ada. I'll be riding with you."

"We need information," suggested Lewis. "Let's ask around

before heading to your place. Maybe we can stir up some information on that bastard before we walk into an ambush," Lewis said as he flicked away the stub of his smoke.

"Lord almighty, y'all are stubborn," Ada grumbled.

The three entered the town via the main street. "Commerce Street," Ada introduced it as.

Upon first glance, all seemed calm and everyone was going on about their business.

Ada noticed fewer folks than she recalled, and most of the ones she saw today she could not place. "Home," she mumbled again, a word as foreign to her as the concept.

The machinations of small-town life were all at work without any obvious troubles. A small gasp escaped Ada's lips when she saw the stable done up with new wood as memories of blood in the dirt street and a man firing down at her flashed in her mind's eye.

The second floor, above the stalls where the horses were kept, was also sided with fresh timbers. A new wide-open window even overlooked the dusty lane.

Peachie looked up at Ada. "That's the spot?" the girl asked.

Ada gestured with a tilt of her head.

Peachie mimicked the nod in silence.

A familiar whistle carried upon the wind to Ada's ears. "Well,

I'll be. If it ain't Miss Picou," came a man's voice.

Johnny Pile stood on the wooden planks at the front of his office and pulled off his hat. He was smiling with a big and toothy grin.

"Damn, they ain't shook ya off yet, Deputy Johnny Pile?" Ada greeted him jovially and tipped her hat to him.

The smile Johnny wore grew, and he proudly placed his thumbs under his suspenders. "Sheriff now, Ada. Lots changed 'round here. Lots stayed the same too, I guess," he stated. "Last time I saw you, I asked you not to come back," his tone shifted slightly as he spoke, and his friendly eyes held a hint of steely seriousness.

Ada frowned. "Yeah, ah know. Ah don't listen so well." She threw Johnny a wry smile.

He looked away and shook his head. "Look, Ada. I don't know if you should be hangin' around these parts. I'm not sure folks who remember will take kindly to your return," he gestured to the repaired stables.

Ada sighed and pulled off her hat. "Ah ain't leavin' jist yet. Ah'm here to see about my ranch and," she squeezed Peachie's hand gently, "finish what ah started."

Johnny met Ada's eye before he cast a furtive glance to the old office of Mr. Guilford Grimshaw. "And who are these folk?" Johnny gestured to Ada's companions with his hat.

Ada hesitated before answering, "Friends."

The sheriff rubbed at his brow and shook his head. "Well, you can come through town, but no trouble. Things are calm in these parts now and it's my job to keep it that way." He cast a leery eye upon Ada before leaning casually against a beam in front of his office.

"Ya wear it well Johnny," Ada complimented him with a slight grin and a bright eye. "Stables look good too," she said.

He paled a bit. "You ain't here to blow nothin' up again, are you?" Still, his tone took on a hesitant and joking air.

Ada shook her head and leaned against the horn while Peachie's arms hung loosely at Ada's hips. "Nah, jist passin' through. We lookin' for someone," she said.

"Well, William's at your ranch," Johnny responded, misunderstanding Ada's comment.

It was a blow to Ada's chest, and she sat back up abruptly. "Is he alright?"

Sheriff Johnny Pile looked down at Ada through tight eyes, "I don't rightly know. He ain't been out here in a while. Honestly, we've been dealing with much around here, with the sicknesses and all." He tilted his head to the inn. "Ms. Peace would know more down at the inn. She's been by and delivered goods to the place on occasion after you left."

Ada nodded, grateful for the information.

"It's been a bad year for all of us," Johnny went on solemnly.

He gestured to the graveyard at the end of the street and Ada saw that it had grown in size. "Welcome back, Ada," he tried to add as cheerfully as he could manage.

She nodded to him and turned the roan—

"Bless my soul!" A woman's surprised yelp filled the street.

Ada spotted an older woman whose kind eyes shone in recognition. "Ms. Peace!" Ada's voice held her raw emotion as she noted that Ms. Peace looked the same as she had when Ada had ridden from town.

The elderly woman's prematurely gray curls, now white, were piled on top of her head and she wore a smart, functional dress and a glowing smile. Mrs. Peace's eyes shone with a bright kindness that put everyone she spoke to at ease as Ada rode the roan over to where Ms. Peace stood on the planked walkway.

Ada swung quickly out of the saddle and was on the porch, hugging the older woman before Peachie could speak. The two women held each in a strong embrace that lingered tenderly and spoke of poignant history."Ms. Peace, it's good to see ya," Ada eventually said.

"My goodness Ada! It's mighty fine seeing you again," Ms. Peace gushed like a mother hen. She emphasized each word as she caught her breath. Ms. Peace held Ada at arm's length, "Let me see you, girl." Worry crossed her face as she took in Ada's haggard visage. "You been riding hard it looks like."

Ada hesitantly nodded.

"You come because you got my letter?" Ms. Peace asked.

The two women held hands for a moment before Ada answered, "Ah did. That's one of the reasons ah'm here."

Miss Peace nodded and looked over at the strangers that had ridden in with Ada. "You have to tell me about your travels. But first," she turned to Peachie, Lewis, and Ezekiel, "who might you two be?"

Peachie spoke up first. "My name is Adelle Durand and I am from France."

Ada added, "I call her Peachie."

Ms. Peace smiled at Ada and nodded to Peachie.

"I'm Zeke," called Ezekiel.

"Lewis, ma'am. Lewis Buchanan from Georgia," Lewis introduced himself, retrieving his military formality from his past.

"They're with me. Been riding since just outside the Dakotas," Ada said.

Ms. Peace looked at her with a mix of surprise and concern. "Well, we'll catch up, after you eat," the kindly old woman stated matter-of-factly. She walked off briskly to the inn and threw back over her shoulder and winked at Ada. "You remember your way I imagine?"

A warm feeling flooded Ada, and she nodded. "Ya know ah do." Ada said, with the shadow of a smile on her face.

"We need to find out if we're walking into a trap," Lewis stated.

"Ms. Peace knows everything that goes on 'round here. She'll know," Ada answered tensely.

The group followed Ms. Peace and tethered the roan and mule to the h-brace outside the inn where a full trough of cold, fresh water sat before them. Peachie gave both animals some corn from a bag, while Ada and Lewis helped Ezekiel up the short stairs and into the inn. Peachie eventually followed the three travelers inside slowly and with trepidation.

The group ate some eggs and bacon as Ada shared her story with the kindly Ms. Peace. The older woman listened and spoke not a word as Ada recounted her trials in the snowy Dakota Territory and her run-ins with the blue-eyed man.

"He shot me in the leg, twice." Ada unconsciously rubbed at her thigh. "Been follow'n him back here and ah reckon he's gun'n for William."

Ms. Peace sat in silence for a time after Ada finished talking before she eventually stood and walked to the kitchen.

Peachie looked at Ada, and the weary woman shrugged under her Stetson at the girl.

Ms. Peace came back with a bottle. "This here was Mr. Peace's," she said as she placed a heavy bottle of bourbon on the table.

"Sorry ma'am we don't have time for that," Lewis stated.

Ms. Peace looked at the soldier. "You don't want to go in blind. Let me speak for a bit before you leave." Ms. Peace looked at Ada when she continued, "Girl, you've been through it."

Ada nodded slowly and looked past Ms. Peace to the large windows in the front of the inn, remembering.

"Ada," she said in a worried tone, "he was here, that man you fought in Mr. Grimshaw's office."

Ada's muscles tightened at the memory and she balled her fists instinctively.

"Was my brother with him?" Peachie asked quickly, interrupting the exchange.

Ms. Peace nodded and frowned. "He had a boy with him. Small with dark hair. I gave the boy some food, but refused to feed *that* man." She gestured to the street. "He worked for that terrible Mr. Minger and I just didn't want him around." Ms. Peace looked to Peachie, "I didn't know that boy was your brother. The sheriff could have arrested that man for kidnapping if I had." She looked about fretfully and placed a motherly hand on Peachie's shoulder.

Ada sighed and shook her head. "Nah, ya couldn't of known

and Johnny'd be dead if he tried anything. Ah'm guess'n he lit out?"

Ms. Peace nodded. "He rode south out of town. There were other men with him. All a surly bunch."

Ada's brow furrowed in confusion and she scrunched up her face. "South?"

Peachie looked at Ada, "Where is he taking my brother?"

Shaking her head in confusion, Ada answered, "Ah don't rightly know." Ada thumbed her jaw and thought about the Preacher, trying to figure his plans.

Ezekiel had finally finished eating and offered, "Maybe he is get'n a posse or friends or somethin."

"*Foire,*" Ada cursed under her breath. "Could be that."

Peachie worried her lip and Ms. Peace looked to the new wood and glass on the front of her building, remembering the destruction that followed Ada before she looked at Peachie with a motherly eye. "So, you and your brother are from France?" she asked.

"Yes, ma'am," Peachie answered.

"Well, bonjour," said Ms. Peace. "Cava?"

Peachie's face was a mixture of surprise and joy and Ada watched on, smiling to herself. It was rare that the girl let slip a smile.

Peachie answered, "Cava bien, et tu?"

"Tres bien," responded Ms. Peace before directing a kind eye at Ada. "Now that Ada's back."

Ada nervously shuffled her boot under the table and looked at the ground. "Thank you, ma'am, for the food," Lewis said as he finished his plate.

Ms. Peace nodded. "I see you've all been starved." She cast her eyes over the stack of plates in front of the men who sat before her.

Ada shifted onto her feet. "Thank ya fer everything." She tapped her hat to Ms. Peace.

Ms. Peace pulled Ada into another hug. "I know I ain't as good a looker as that William, but you better stop in more now that you're back in town." She sniffled and a tissue appeared as she dabbed at her eyes.

"Is he alright?" Ada asked.

Ms. Peace looked Ada dead in the eyes and shook her head. "He ain't his best, but he will be now that you're back."

Ada nodded and looked at the ground before whispering, "Can the girl stay here?"

"I will not," Peachie spoke harshly. The young girl hopped to her feet and glared at Ada. "I will get my brother back."

Ms. Peace looked at Ada. "She is welcome to stay," then quickly added, "when her brother is safe. When They both are."

Ada sighed and tightened her lips.

"Ada, the girl is safer with you. If that man comes back, well, there isn't much I can do," Ms. Peace said.

"Alright kid, ya can ride with me," Ada stated, her decision made.

"Oh, one more thing, Ada," Ms. Peace pulled Ada in close to speak low. "Some woman's come through town looking for your place. She was tall and had black hair. Spoke in a clipped and eastern kinda way. I didn't take to her none, so I sent her in the opposite direction."

Ada cursed. "Athena."

"Who?" Ms. Peace quirked her brow.

Ada narrowed her eyes and looked out into the street, half expecting to see the merchant, and senator's wife, on her wagon. "Nuthin, jist a bad memory. It'll be alright," Ada answered in an attempt to relieve the older woman's concerns.

Ada, Peachie, Lewis, and Ezekiel stepped out into the sunshine. The town was full of the movement of horses and townsfolk as a soft breeze blew through, sending the mingling smells of sawdust and the wilds down the street.

"Home," Ada tried out the word again. It had started to feel better on her tongue.

As the quartet stepped along the hard-planked walkway, they saw the horse and mule were gone.

"What the hell?" Ada asked incredulously as she stepped off the wood and onto the dirt road. Her face was growing red and Peachie gasped.

A man and his wife darted away from Ada down an alley whispering to one another.

"Look over yonder," Lewis pointed to the stable.

Ada turned and spotted the red roan and the mule. Someone was saddling them to ride. Storming over to the stable, Ada's eyes took in the brushed coats and clean leathers. "Hey," she called to the stable boy. She was stunned into silence by the boy when he turned around. He was a little older than Peachie and stood almost at Ada's height. "Abel!"

He smiled broadly and put his hand out to Ada, and she took his small hand in hers and shook it. Peachie stepped back into Lewis, who rested a hand on her shoulder. Ezekiel watched on in confusion as Ada held the hand of the boy and a flood of memories shot into her mind. Images of his Mexican sister, Therese Martinez, and the struggles the two women shared washed over her.

Abel was beaming with a beautiful smile of white teeth. "I took care of the horse," he said.

Ada nodded and patted his back as another wave of warm feelings cascaded over her. "Maybe, ah'm home after all," she whispered. "Thank ya Abel. This here is Peachie, and this fella is Zeke. That gruff old timer is Lewis," Ada introduced her companions. She caught Peachie blushing slightly and gave her a wry smile.

Abel smiled. "Welcome back. I'm running to help Joseph now. He's our new butcher. We are building his house."

"Ah smelled it on the wind, love the smell of fresh cut wood," Ada said as she watched Abel dart off down an alley. She shook her head at the changes and growth of the town.

After leaving Ms. Peace's and the stable behind, Ada's next stop was the bank. It was a small bank with a small safe, but Ada's bounty money from years of struggle had been parked there. The teller was a man she did not recognize.

"Ada Picou," the man stated incredulously.

"Y'all got my money?" Ada asked.

The teller pulled Ada's information and revealed that much of her funds had been depleted due to the restoration of the town.

"Hot smack a rabbit," Ada exclaimed.

"The town confiscated some of your funds to repair the stable. I heard you blew it up," the teller said coolly.

Ada's eyes darted to Peachie and found the girl staring open-mouthed. "Well, yeah, sumthin' like that," Ada answered. She pulled some coin aside for Abel to thank him for tending the horses.

"I will see to it that young Abel receives this," the banker stated.

Ada tipped her hat and smiled her thanks.

The three then walked over to stock up at Mr. Carter's general store, where a few people openly stared at Ada.

"Got lots of friends here," Lewis said sarcastically.

"Well, it was a rough patch," Ada replied.

"Ada Picou, it is good to see you again," said Mr. Carter as the group walked in the door.

She responded in kind, "It's good to see ya too Mr. Carter."

"Pish posh," he waved her away, smiling. "Just call me James," he said with a wink.

She noticed that his smile lines had deepened and his slight stoop had grown.

Mr. Carter helped Lewis and Ezekiel fill the saddlebags and added a few extra things for the mule. "How about that new stable you bought us?" Mr. Carter asked.

"Ah saw it. Looks mighty fine. Worth every darn penny," Ada

smiled, feeling a bit conflicted.

"Glad to have you on our side," Mr. Carter added.

Ada tapped her marbled Stetson to the general store owner.

"Have you seen William?" Mr. Carter asked.

Ada shook her head with a look of concern as the conversation shifted. "Head'n there now."

The old man nodded to her. "He did more than I realized for me."

Ada sighed, "Me too, James. Me too."

"Ada," Mr. Carter called to her as she was leaving. "A Ms. Whitmore called while you've been away. Rode in on a loaded wagon. Said she was heading to your old place." Mr. Carter shook his head in consternation, "I think Ms. Peace intentionally sent her in the wrong direction, if you're waiting on her."

Ada smiled and shrugged. "Me and Ms. Athena Whitmore have a bit of a history ya could say. Hope she keeps head'n the wrong way and finds someone else to bother," Ada said as she led the roan away from the general store and departed the town.

Riding the familiar route to the ranch she had built with William, Ada thought back to the town she had just left. The people treated her kindly as she rode through town, although she noted some were understandably a little chilly. "Ah earned it, ah s'pose," she said low and to herself. A few cool eyes reminded her of the damage she wrought and, as she sat upon the red roan with Peachie at her back, she tilted her head up to the sky.

It was a flat blue expanse full of possibilities.

"Where is this ranch o' yers at?" Ezekiel asked after they had ridden a day on the familiar route to her place.

"We'll be there soon," Ada answered.

"Didn't want to be too close to civilization, right?" Lewis asked.

Ada nodded and gave a halfhearted shrug. "Yer right there." "Yer sure ya don't want to wait fer Henri back there in town, with Ms. Peace?" Ada asked the girl.

Peachie bit her lip and answered firmly, "That man is looking to hurt you. I'm staying by your side. Sorry Ada. Ms. Peace was right."

Ada shrugged, knowing that she would lose this argument. "Sounds like yer using me as bait. . ." Ada considered.

"She is," Lewis interjected.

Peachie shrugged back at Ada and cocked an eyebrow in a mirthful way. "Maybe I am."

Ezekiel chuckled occasionally at the turns Ada and Peachie took at one another.

"Hush ya piraque, ah'll send Peachie back on that mule and ya can walk the rest of the way," Ada said.

"Alright, alright, I'll stop listening. As best I can." Ezekiel raised a hand in his defense.

"What Ada, you want me to walk too?" shot Lewis in indignation when Ada shifted her glare his way. "This is my derned mule anyhow," he concluded in a huff.

Ada shook her head in mild frustration.

The next day, Ada tried reasoning again, "Ah ain't got not a sign on him."

Peachie shook her head, "You're not dead yet, so I think he will turn up."

Ezekiel added, "He knows what you got to lose. And he know yer determined not to let 'em go."

Ada turned to Ezekiel with a look that was ready and coiled to strike.

Both of Ezekiel's hands flew up. "N-Now, now—" he stammered. "I didn't mean no harm," the man said quickly.

Ada was red and her temper had flared before abating just as fast. "It ain't ya, ah know it. It's that damn creature, been dogging me my whole life seems," Ada explained.

"Ada, he is right. That's why he has my brother too. He is looking to hurt people. Especially you, and those you care about," Peachie observed.

Ada's fists, tight and shaking, fell to her sides, limp. "We gotta git there first is all," she said, desperation tainting her voice.

Peachie and Ezekiel nodded in a mutual expression of worry.

"We'll get him, Ada," Lewis said as he cleaned his gun and checked his rounds.

That last night, on the trail between town and Ada's land, Peachie spoke to Ezekiel in private.

"You didn't do anything wrong. Ada is just worried about what she will find at her ranch," Peachie explained.

"Woman's a lot like Jebediah," he said sadly.

Peachie patted the man's arm and softly bobbed her head in agreement.

CHAPTER NINETEEN

A heavy silence, pregnant with the promise of suffering, rode with the travelers, with none of the four riders uttering a sound. The mule set the pace with Ezekiel and Peachie on its back, while Ada sat atop the tall roan where she could cast her tight glance across the long horizon.

Peachie's eyes wandered constantly over Ada and the horizon beyond. Ms. Peace and Mr. Carter had allowed them food, rest, and supplies. They also filled Ada's head with hope, and with worry. William had not been to town and had asked everyone to stay away, being worried about being contagious. Ada knew William had developed the cough that had been ravaging the countryside, thanks to the information shared by Ms. Peace.

"Damn martyr," Ada cursed the man under her breath. She worried her lip. "It ain't far," she said absently under her breath.

It had been at least a year since she had made the trek, yet she still knew it by heart.

"I'm sure your William is alright, Ada." Peachie tried to bring Ada a little comfort with her sincere words of encouragement. However, the words sounded hollow and Peachie looked to the dry dusty earth as she rode, knowing that her attempts were in vain and that anything she said only fell upon deaf ears.

The weary companions rode into the familiar valley as the sun was setting itself upon the western peaks.

"Home," Ada breathed, the word barely audible as she took in the sight before her.

Sitting behind Ada, Peachie heard the words and felt the familiar weight that they carried. The red roan stamped in excitement and flicked his tail in recognition. He knew this land well and picked up his step as he made his way back to the world he knew best.

Upon further entering the valley, Ada knew immediately something was wrong. "The grass is high." She looked bewilderedly across the empty expanse ahead of her and mumbled, "Where are the cattle?" Her eyes narrowed in suspicion.

Confusion, anger, and worry struggled within Ada for dominance. Bramble-covered weeds had even grown up in the garden, and the stalls were in disrepair. Boards hung loose, and gaps showed through the roofing.

The quarter horse Ada had left behind ran from the empty pasture to greet the roan with a familiar sniff and he chuffed eagerly at her. The little horse had cracks and splays in her hooves as well as matted, dirty fur. The mule shied away from the quarter horse. Ada watched and Lewis struggled to keep it steady.

Ada's worry increased at the sight of the unkempt, socialization-starved horse. "William," she muttered in concern.

Showdown

The stone home she and William had built still stood.
However, it looked abandoned and, like everything else in the
valley, forgotten. At the front of the small building, the door
hung, still attached but ajar.

Ada swung down from the saddle and threw the reins across
the brace outside the house. Her eyes did not stray from the
darkened doorway as she cautiously approached the home and
undid the safety thong on her right pistol.

Movement and a figure standing in the darkness startled her.
Soon, however, she made out the form of William emerging
slowly as he peered through the doorway and leaned partly
against the doorjamb.

They both stood in shock and surprise as they beheld each
other. A tumult of emotions raged within Ada, and she moved
swiftly to the exhausted-looking man before her who threw
open his arms and just as eagerly received her. Tears welled up
in their eyes. An eternity passed, and they stood as one.

Ada leaned back and looked into William's eyes. She was lost
again. The only way she wanted to be lost again. Longing to be
lost in his gaze.

Ada shifted to kiss him, and William braced his arms to keep
her back, not quite ready to fully relax in their reunion. "You
know I was sick a while back, Ada," he said with worry and
longing in his eyes.

Ada pushed between his wobbly arms and firmly placed her
lips upon his. They shared a kiss that brightened the valley and
put them into the clouds. Ada could feel William's heartbeat.

Showdown

Her heart raced, and the world spun. William, giving in despite his martyr's spirit, held Ada in his strong and steady hands.

Peachie, Ezekiel, and Lewis looked away as they each turned a shade of pink.

CHAPTER TWENTY

The small group of adults gathered around the fire as Peachie proudly took care of the animals. She stalled the mule, red roan, and the quarter horse in what remained of the stable. All three animals had been hayed, brushed, and their hooves had been trimmed.

Ada caught the young girl peeking her way occasionally. "Ya look jealous or sumthin' there, girl."

"You are wrong," Peachie responded curtly as she finished her work and joined the others at the fire. "So, this is William."

"The one and only," replied a slightly lighter-in-mood Ada.

The young girl's countenance shifted. "Well, you're going to catch whatever he has," Peachie observed.

"I'm okay. Been better for a couple of weeks. Just left me tired, is all," William answered.

The dark circles were plain as day under William's eyes.

"Got everything stove up. I know the feeling," Lewis interjected.

"We still are all going to die," Peachie huffed hopelessly. "Just as my parents and brother are dead," she added as her sour gaze wandered to the dark ridgeline in the distance.

Ada looked at Peachie. "Ya think he's close?"

Peachie picked at her shoe. "Probably is close. We are here, aren't we, at your ranch? This is where he's been leading us, or racing us, or whatever, as you've said." Peachie was turning red as she spoke, and her voice cracked. "I need my brother to be okay, but I just don't know if you all are enough," the doubt in the young girl's voice wrapped her words.

The words stung Ada and Lewis, and they visibly flinched.

"I know I'm old, girl, but I been through war. I got what it takes. You don't need to fear none," the old soldier reassured her.

"Peachie, ah been collecting bounties since ah was not much older than ya. This man is evil, but he's still a man and ah've made him bleed," Ada spoke solemnly.

"I've got a shotgun here and a lot of shells. It would take a small army to make it through us," William added while trying to contribute to the conversation.

"I want him dead too, Peachie. He's got to pay for laying Jebediah low," the simple man spoke softly his voice saturated in emotion.

"I just want to bastard dead for what he's done to you and your brother," Lewis added. "Promise of coin helps too," he laughed mirthfully.

"We all have a reason to hate the man," William said while

soberly looking at Ada.

"A few of us are good enough shots," Lewis said with hope lacing his voice, still trying to brighten the mood.

"We're not dead yet. Hold on to whatever hope you can fit in your hand, Peachie. You know Lewis is really good shot," Ezekiel added.

William nodded and wore a look of concern for the young girl as Ada sighed and poked at the fire with a stick.

Ada recognized the tone in the girl's voice. It was one she herself had borne for years after the Preacher killed her family. "Ah know yer feelin' hopeless girl, but ya have us. There is still hope." Ada spoke the words she wished she could have heard herself as a youth.

William scratched at his growing beard. "Ada, I don't know where to start—" he coughed.

"William, don't push yerself. We'll catch up after a while," Ada said with rare gentleness. She looked past him into the darkness with worry clear upon her face. "We got to ready ourselves. My gut says that." One question nagged at her though. "Where are the head?"

"Sold 'em off and was planning on starting up again." William's body shook with a coughing fit after he spoke.

Ada nodded. "You been busy out here."

He waved her away. "That's bullshit and you know it. It looks like hell. I was keeping up 'till this damn cough grabbed me."

Again, Ada nodded with worry plain in her eyes. "Well, ah'm glad ya was here at least."

"I passed the bar, Ada," William said in an attempt to shift their minds to a more neutral topic. Everyone was still, and nobody responded.

"You shit what?" asked Ezekiel after a moment.

Peachie turned red with embarrassment. And Ada looked incredulous, her glare dubious. Lewis choked on his coffee, spitting some out and spraying his dusty shirt.

"No, no, no," William said quickly. "I'm a lawyer now. I passed the test. It's called a bar test," William explained.

Ezekiel shook his head, his eyes wide in bewilderment. "That so? Congratulations then."

Ada smiled and wore a proud expression. "Ah knew ya could do it."

"Couldn't have done it without—"

Both William and Ada's gazes meandered toward the ground as they recalled Mr. Guilford Grimshaw, the man who had helped them both so much.

Mr. Grimshaw, the same man who had accepted and trusted Ada, had helped William obtain his lawyer status. That same man was now buried in the town graveyard along with a good deal of other townspeople. Notions of death played across their imaginations, and the mood quickly grew somber.

Peachie broke the silence. "Where's your dog Ada? The one you said you had?"

"Yeah, where is that ol' dog. . . ?" Ada cast her eyes around the homestead and spotted no dog.

"He lit out a bit after I caught this croop," William said as he looked to the spot where the dog used to lay.

"Ah see. . . ah think we done enough catching up fer one night," Ada stated, shutting down the fireside talk.

Lewis and Ezekiel, taking the cue, started picking up.

"I'll set my bedroll in the stable," Ezekiel said as he walked off into the cool darkness.

"I guess I'm with him," Lewis added as he grabbed his saddle and walked toward the stalls.

Peachie chewed her lip as she watched the adults scatter.

"You two are welcome—" William stopped himself and turned to Ada. "I really don't think I can get you sick anymore. It's been near a month since the fever left me and I burned everything I was wearing," he said reassuringly.

Ada's eyes went to the young girl whose face was creased with concern. "Much obliged, but us gals will bunk under the stars tonight," Ada said. She glanced at Peachie and gave her a small nod.

The girl sighed with relief.

William scratched at his shoulder. "Alright. I didn't change anything, Ada," he added.

She responded with a soft-eyed, quiet look laden with unspoken thoughts and an understated smile as the night waxed on.

The quiet of a pale, golden sunrise erupted into violence and gunfire while the grass was still slick with dew. Chaos thrust all five people on the homestead into action As the thundering of hooves announced the early morning arrival of the Preacher and his posse.

As Ada had heard in town, the Preacher indeed rode in with a gang of unruly men.

"Ada Picou!" The Preacher called out, "I'm arrived and here to see you dead!" He bellowed into the morning air.

Ada, groggy and disoriented, grabbed Peachie from the bedroll and pulled her into the safety of the nearby stone shack.

"Damn you woman, come out a face me. I'll lay you low the way your grandpappy did my pa!" the Preacher yelled at the building as Ada slid her .44 Colts from the leathers.

"William!" Ada yelled as she scanned the main house for signs of movement.

Peachie was already poised with the Spencer and had the stock in her shoulder. Ada could only hope Ezekiel and Lewis were awake and ready, holding their positions quietly in the stalls.

"Peachie—!" a small voice cried out.

Ada's head snapped around to look at the girl, and the blood drained from her face.

Peachie met Ada's eyes, and the woman shook her head.

"He bait'n ya," she growled low. Ada stood to her full height and sighed. After putting her hat on, she holstered her pistols and adjusted her belt. She walked out into the sun through the damaged door and rested a hand on Peachie's shoulder for a moment as she went.

The man Ada hunted was here, and she intended to meet his challenge.

"Ah'm here," Ada called out. Her eyes quickly adjusted to the morning glare as, standing in the doorway, she saw the man with the piercing blue eyes.

The Preacher glared at her, his rawboned face a mess of lacerations. "Keep your hands where I can see 'em, I don't trust no Picous," he spoke with disgust as the venom dripped from his voice.

As the two squared off, Ada looked over at the small boy held hostage in the Preacher's lap. He was seven or eight and had soft, curly hair that looked just like Peachie's. Ada noted a wild look about him, but being with the Preacher had understandably left the child malnourished, mistreated, and disheveled. Her heart ached for his safety.

"Remind you of someone," the Preacher taunted Ada with an evil grin when he saw her weakly eyeing the boy. He stole a quick glance around with teeth bared. "Athena is going to like this place, even with a full graveyard on the property," the Preacher said condescendingly. He spat into the grass below his horse.

Ada stood, muscles taut and ready for any opening for her to release hellfire on the demon. But the boy was in the way and she could do the Preacher no harm until he was safe. Time slowed, and as the tension grew, someone fired the first shot.

Ada dove to the ground as puffs of dust popped at her heels in an arc. She lunged behind a large protruding rock, finding temporary cover as, like lightning, Ada had both Colts out and firing into the din.

The large black horse under the man started and, with eyes wildly rolling as the horse arched up on its hind legs and thrashed out, his hooves slid across the wet grass. The Preacher and Henri slid out of the saddle and onto the damp ground below as the horse lost its footing and followed its riders to the ground beside them.

Ada spotted Henri as he fell away from the horse, his body landing in a small and crumpled heap atop the hard ground. On her belly, Ada crawled over to him quickly and noticed that bullets were blazing from the stalls.

Ada twisted her head and glimpsed William carefully firing into the churning dust as men yelled, guns stabbed, fire blazed, and horses snorted. The small stone house became perforated and pockmarked with bullets as a rebel yell erupted from somewhere behind her and Ada saw Lewis, brandishing a rope, tearing a man down from his horse.

Lurching to the small boy in the wet grass, Ada caught a bullet in her arm. Blackness and stars welled into Ada's vision as it wracked her body with pain. Suddenly, a wet yell erupted from the stalls.

Through the sweat and dirt in her eyes, Ada saw both her roan and the quarter horse go down just outside the stall openings, their dirt and hooves flying in a mad dash with no chance of escaping what pursued them. Her eyes, bloodshot and heart racing as she bit, back tears and strained against her instinct to bolt to her horse, add to her pain as Ada feels the loss of her steadfast companion. She spotted Ezekiel in the stable with his back against the wall as three men of the posse opened fire into him, their guns flashing with bloody horror that burned into Ada's mind.

A guttural yell escaped Ada's dry and cracked lips just as a final bullet from Ezekiel's dying hand and takes one of the men in the head. His body jerked and flopped to one side, the grass near him painting itself red after possibly the only straight shot the man ever made.

The other two men darted away for cover only to stumble into Lewis's Winchester repeater rifle and are blasted with fire and smoke. Ada's veins are bulged in her neck as her mind tried to process the loss of her horse and the kindly man who had traveled by her side.

Like a viper, the Preacher sprung upon Ada and tried to suffocate her with his fury. Using a fierce pull, he yanked her off of the small French boy and the two enemies toppled together, sliding in the wet grass as Ada and the Preacher, both bloody and mired in filth, struggled against one another. Their bodies rolled and tangled together as each struggled to strike at the other.

Both of the children vanished from Ada's view as she struggled with the man with the deathly blue eyes. All she could see was the man before her that killed her mother, father, and brother. She heard William's shotgun as though it were miles away, the rate of gunfire seeming to slow near the two bodies locked in mortal combat.

Somewhere in the valley of fury and death, Ada heard curses and anger from the surviving men that had ridden in with the Preacher. William and the children must have been trapped in the small home Ada built, and she is aware of it.

Renewed gunfire echoed through the valley and bounced off the ridges and rolled back into the sway of the field. The cacophony made it impossible for Ada to know who was firing and from where.

The keening wails of men pierced the surrounding air as Ada and the Preacher continued to roll as one across the moist earth, grappling on the ground. Neither the Preacher nor Ada were able to grasp and wield a weapon. Their bodies careened into the creek near the homestead as elbows jabbed into flesh, knees landed hits on either's stomach, and both sprayed curses from their busted lips.

Ada raked her nails like claws at the Preacher's face, making him a nightmare of sweat, mud, and blood.

Incoherently, the two threw curses at each other as they hungrily gasped for breath. Fists flew between them, striking muscle and bone. Kicks desperately flailed and nails scraped at raw flesh.

Ada's eyes took in the mad desperation and hatred in the cold, inhuman blue eyes of the man trying to kill her and she swore she could see her own reflection mirrored the same in his.

Flecks of spittle and blood frothed at the edges of their mouths. Matted and discolored, their hair and clothes became unrecognizable in the fray. The copper smell and taste of blood-filled Ada's senses.

Her eyes widened as she felt the Preacher's hands on her throat. His eyes were death and she could see that all reason had departed the man. Large and calloused hands slid in the wetness coating Ada's skin and made slurping noises as the Preacher tried to squeeze the life from Ada.

Choking and gurgling, Ada struggled to find a breath. She straddled the ground, her body twisted with the Preacher's above her in the soft mud and sodden gravel. Her arms and legs kicked out and slid wildly in the muck, leaving shallow ruts that filled quickly with water.

She felt her eyes bulging in her skull and the heat of her red-hot face. Her mind blanked and became nothing but instinctual desperation for survival. For an instant, Ada and the Preacher's eyes met. Ada could see tears streaming his face, but she had no opportunity for thought or confusion as to why.

The Preacher stammered out a curse in her ear, his mouth so close that she could hear the saliva crackling. "Damn you and your blood to hell!"

His words broke her from the spell that held Ada. She realized incredulously that he was sobbing as he choked her. A calm stillness overcame her as blackness closed in on her. Hopelessness spread across Ada as she thought about the family she could not avenge And, through the blackness, she saw the Preacher's face above her twisted into a mask of pure rage and hate.

A shot rang out and the evil man's body shook above Ada. The grip on Ada's throat loosened as the Preacher cried sharply in pain. Out of the corner of her eye, Ada saw Peachie standing with the smoking Spencer held high.

Tears run down the young girl's face, but they are not the tears of the defeated.

"Ya done pissed off one too many folk," Ada grunted through clenched teeth.

The woman seized the moment and shot out a hidden blade with one hand, striking the Preacher's carotid artery. There was a small moment when Ada felt his grip slip in the wet grime. Lurching into him, she threw her head between his arms and tore herself from his grip.

Twisting her wet and battered body, Ada snaked over him and used all of her weight and the last of her strength to shove the wild man's head into the soft creek bed.

The Preacher's sputters and cries roiled in Ada's ears as Ada shoved hard on his head and straddled his hips.

The Preacher spasmodically jerked in all directions, trying to find purchase in the slippery earth. He struggled and failed to reach her or lift her, his limbs slipping uselessly in the wetness.

All Ada was aware of was their bodies trapped together and her desperation to hold the Preacher in place. Ada was unable to see his face in the muddy sludge, only able to perceive the brown and gray mire that filled all of his creases and scars.

Ada had no sense of time. She had no idea how long the Preacher lay still as she held her spot with muscles shaking until she became sick upon his back. Heaving, she fell over and away from him. Her eyes peered at him through blood and filth.

The Preacher remained still.

The sound of gunfire faded and was replaced with the loud thrumming of Ada's heart. Ada looked at the Preacher, his body still and pale, through her shaking and blood-covered fingers.

Her body convulsed as she fell to her back. The wide open blue sky was all that remained in her view, a view filled with limitless possibilities.

A feeling like falling into the void surrounded Ada, and the next moment she was weightless.

EPILOGUE

Athena gestured with a dismissive wave to Ada and William as they left the homestead they had built together.

"Didn't figure she'd make it back this way. Thought someone would put the old snake down," Ada stated in frustration and disappointment.

William's shoulders sagged a bit as he said, "Everything was legal, though."

Ada nodded tightly, her lips drawn into a thin white line.

Ada and William stopped in the town before leaving to pay their respects to the dead.

"He was the first to accept me round here," she told William as they stood before the gravestone of the man they both owed, at least in part, their present lives to. The grave was not yet fully covered in grass and the stone was new, the edges still sharp.

William nodded and added, "He was a good one like that, always could spot someone's true worth

The stone with Guilford Grimshaw's name depicted the range spanning the man's too short years.

Ada stood quietly, without knowing what to say, as a tear dripped out onto the dry dust at her feet. A few birds nearby twittered and marked the passing of time as Ada shifted uncomfortably from foot to foot and remembered the gentleman lawyer who took a chance on her.

It startled her when a small hand pushed its way into Ada's. Looking down, she saw Peachie's steady eyes on the grave marker of Mr. Grimshaw. Together, they stood wrapped in a heavy blanket of silence.

Lewis walked up to the two and joined the quiet memorial. A soft voice broke the silence and Ada knitted her brow in confusion as the voice grew louder. Ada realized Peachie was praying in French using words she had heard herself as a child in the bayous of the Atchafalaya. She did not recognize all the words, but she had heard the prayer before, said slightly differently by her mother.

Ada's breath caught, and she glanced at Lewis to find him wearing an expression of utter sadness that made him look even older than his rough years. There were dark circles under his eyes and his face was a map of scars. They all wept softly until the three spoke together, following Peachie's prayer, saying:

"Amen."

Ada glanced to Ezekiel's grave not far from where they stood and tipped her hat to his marker.

Peachie and Henri stood with Ada and William on the porch of Ms. Peace's inn.

"Y'all will be alright with Ms. Peace," Ada said to the children as Ms. Peace nodded along beside them.

Peachie held her brother's hand tightly, and the smiling boy gladly accepted her doting. "

I will take care of them, Ada, as though they were my own," Ms. Peace stated.

Ada nodded and smiled. "Ah know ya will."

Peachie put an arm around her brother and wept softly, nodding.

Lewis encountered Ada outside of the general store, the man's arms empty of goods.

"Well, where ya head'n now," Ada asked the old soldier.

He sighed, his eyes dark and sunken. "I might stay a bit around here. See if they got any need for an old codger," Lewis said, smiling softly. "I don't think I'm quite ready to light a shuck just yet," he said with a heavy heart.

Ada shook the old man's hand. "You'll like it here. Usually a peaceful town, ah reckon. Ms. Peace is a damn fine cook to boot," Ada said, trying to lift the man's spirits.

"Yeah, I saw a few things that could use fixin over there. Think she's in need of a handyman?" He gestured to the inn.

Ada nodded and smiled.

Showdown

William sat on his horse, waiting for Ada as she climbed stiffly onto the red roan.

"Well, Miss Picou, where are we headed?" William asked her with a smile playing at the corners of his mouth.

Ada tilted her head, considering his question. She met his eyes and smiled. "Don't matter none, lets jist ride together a spell and see where we end up."

ACKNOWLEDGMENTS

This series would not exist if not for the support of my family and friends. Thanks to my parents, Nicky and Patricia and my sister Kelly for believing in me. Thank you Shannon, Gabriele, Sasha, Leyla, Mina, Xander, and Henry for your love, support, enthusiasm and patience.

Thank you, Jamie Johns, my editor, who has endured entirely too much with my submissions. Thank you, Mina Perkins, for the perfect cover art. Your talent captures the adventurous spirit of the West. Thank you, Alex McKenna, whose voice inspired me to write Ada's story.

I would also like to thank our amazing librarians whose strength, resilience, and positivity have been an inspiration for me.

ABOUT THE ARTIST

Cover by:

Mina Perkins

antimina.carrd.co

About the Author

A. B. Parr lives in southeast Louisiana surrounded by family and friends. He enjoys all facets of the Western genre and is always looking for ways to expand upon the mythos of the American frontier. His hobbies include reading, biking, hiking, and listening to music. The author holds degrees in History, Special Education, and Behavioral Psychology.

www.abparr.com
TWIT (X): @abparr_
IG: abparr

———— ★ · ☆ · ★ ————